SNAPSHOTS

Snapshots

A collection of short stories

by

DON TASSONE

Charlotte,

Thank you for all your support of my writing.

Warmly,

Don

Adelaide Books
New York / Lisbon
2021

SNAPSHOTS
A collection of short stories
By Don Tassone

Published by Adelaide Books, New York / Lisbon
adelaidebooks.org

Editor-in-Chief
Stevan V. Nikolic

For any information, please address Adelaide Books
at info@adelaidebooks.org
or write to:
Adelaide Books
244 Fifth Ave. Suite D27
New York, NY, 10001

ISBN: 978-1-955196-90-1

Printed in the United States of America

For my friends

"I am a passionate lover of the snapshot because, of all photographic images, it comes closest to truth."

— Lisette Model

Contents

Acknowledgements

I want to thank my wife, Liz, Kathy Kennedy, Patti Normile, Anna Gayford, Andi Rogers and Nina Bressau for their helpful feedback on various stories in this collection.

I also want to thank Terri Barbush for the beautiful photos which illustrate each of the five themed sections of stories in this collection and Tim Poirier for designing the front cover, working with Terri's photos.

Finally, I want to extend grateful acknowledgement to the editors of *Friday Flash Fiction, TreeHouse Arts Magazine, Bright Flash Literary Review, 101 Words, Scarlet Leaf Review, Free Flash Fiction, Literary Yard, Down in the Dirt Magazine, Mused Literary Review, The Zodiac Review, Red Fez Magazine* and *Flatbush Review*, the online literary magazines where the original versions of many of these stories appeared.

Don Tassone

Preface

Short stories are like snapshots. They're modest. They don't attempt to convey everything, only a moment in time, a fragment of a broader canvas.

But there's a certain truth in snapshots, and sometimes that is enough.

Don Tassone
May 2020

HOPE

Theo

It is a confusing, anxious time. People distant from one another, wearing masks. People worried about their health and their livelihoods. People worried about the future.

You weren't due for another eight weeks. That was the plan anyway.

But you arrived when the time was right, and you were healthy and beautiful and perfect.

Your name is Theo, which means God. We were waiting for you, and you came when we needed you most.

You remind us God is with us. You remind us that, even in a chaotic and perilous time, life finds a way and joy abounds.

Outsider

All his life, Travis had felt like an outsider.

As a kid, he was always the last one picked on teams. As a teenager, he felt unattractive and never went on dates. As an adult, at work, he always seemed to get the least interesting, least important assignments.

It was as if he was not really part of the world. Travis felt more like a spectator, as if he were looking in on the action from the bleacher seats.

One morning, Travis was shaving. He hated looking at himself in the mirror. But that morning, as he scanned his face, Travis paused and looked into his eyes.

He looked beyond their shape, size and color. He looked inside his eyes, and he caught a glimpse of someone he had not seen before. He saw a good man, a man who had been hidden by insecurities, afraid to venture out, a man the world did not know.

Travis stepped back and took a fresh look at himself. For the first time, he did not see himself as unattractive or marginal. For the first time, he saw his true self.

That day, Travis no longer felt like an outsider. He began to feel part of the world because he had begun to see everything, including himself, from the inside.

Reconciled

It took me a while to find your keys. I guess I should have known they would be in your purse, but I'd never looked in your purse, and I forgot where you always kept it: on your chair in the dining room. I don't go in there much anymore.

The first thing I did when I got in your Blazer was turn off the radio. NPR. You were always listening to news. Used to drive me crazy.

An opened pack of Virginia Slims lay on the passenger's seat. Your only vice. I wish you had stopped. I picked up the cigarettes and slipped them into my jacket pocket.

I'd never been to Ray's. I was going to take your car to my place, but I know you really liked Ray. Said he always treated you with respect. So I figured I'd let the guy tune up your car one last time before I sell it.

"May I help you?" said a burly man in dark blue coveralls.

His soft voice and careful diction didn't match his body. He was standing behind the counter, wiping his hands with a rag, having just come in from the garage.

"Good morning," I said. "I'm here for a tune-up on my wife's car."

"And you are?"

"Warren Herbert."

"Oh, Mr. Herbert. I'm sorry. I'm Ray," he said, extending his hand.

"Good to meet you," I said, taking it.

"Your wife hasn't been in for a while."

He doesn't know, I thought. I guess I should have told him, but I'd grown weary of telling people.

"Yeah, well, I thought I'd take care of it for her."

"That's very thoughtful," he said. "May I have the keys?"

"Here you go," I said, handing them over. "It's right out there."

"Great. I'll get right on it. Should take me about an hour. You're welcome to wait here. There's a coffee shop across the street. Your wife usually waits over there."

"I'll wait here," I said.

Turning around, I could see why you waited at the coffee shop. The "waiting room" for customers was small, with only three chairs made of hard plastic. A table in the corner was covered with car magazines. Vending machines took up one wall. A black rug, which was more like a mat, covered most of the grey linoleum floor.

I was the only one there. I slipped a dollar bill into a vending machine that dispensed coffee and hot chocolate. Sipping my so-called coffee, I wished I'd gotten the hot chocolate.

I was flipping through one of the magazines when a young woman came in with a small boy. She was quite short with a broad nose, dark complexion and double eyelids. I knew she was from Vietnam. I felt my heart beat faster and the hair on the back of my neck bristle.

"Good morning," she said, walking by me to the counter.

I just nodded.

The young boy was holding her hand. He was looking at me. He had the woman's round face and black hair, but his eyes were bigger and his skin much lighter. His father must be white, I thought.

Ray came in from the garage. I didn't mean to eavesdrop, but I could hear the woman say she was there for a tune-up too.

Seeing the boy holding her hand reminded me of our kids holding your hand when they were little. That seemed so long ago.

The woman came over and sat down two chairs over. The little boy climbed up on the chair between us. He looked up at me.

"William, can you say good morning?" the woman said.

"Good morning," the boy said, leaning against his mother.

"Your son?" I asked.

"Yes."

"And his name is William?"

"Yes."

"That's a good name."

"Thank you. We named him after your President Bill Clinton."

"Is that right?"

"Yes. He re-established relations between our countries."

"You mean with Vietnam."

"Yes. That is my home country."

I just nodded.

"Have you been there?" she asked.

"Yes."

"I'm from Ho Chi Minh City. Maybe you've been there."

"When I was there, it was called Saigon."

"I see," she said.

"Have you been here long?" I asked.

"About five years."

"What brought you here, if you don't mind me asking."

"No, it's fine. I came to the US with my husband."

"Is he American?"

"Yes."

"From around here?"

"No, he's from California, but we moved here because we couldn't afford to live in California."

"I understand."

"This is a nice place, and we wanted to raise a family here."

"I see. Do you have other children?"

"No, just William, so far."

The boy pointed to one of the vending machines and asked his mother if he could have some candy. They stepped over to the machine, and she bought him a Kit Kat bar. Sitting back down, she unwrapped it, and the boy took a big bite.

"What about you?" she asked.

"Pardon me?"

"Do you have children?"

"Oh, yes. We have two."

"How wonderful. We hope to have at least one more too."

I nodded and looked down at William. His mouth was covered with chocolate.

I thought of Jason and Heather as kids, sitting in their high chair, and how their faces were always covered with food. What a mess they made. That bothered me. I didn't have much patience with the kids. You, on the other hand, were patient to a fault. Maybe that's why the kids always preferred you over me.

Maybe I shouldn't be surprised they haven't called me. I guess their thoughts are still with you.

Of course, I haven't called them either. I'm sure you're not happy about that.

But then I had a knack for upsetting you. You sure hated the Blazer. You wanted a RAV4, but I told you I wouldn't have anything made in Asia under our roof. When you said you'd park it in the driveway, I didn't speak to you for days.

William looked up at me and smiled. Now he had chocolate in his hair.

The woman laughed.

"Oh, William!" she said.

She pulled a pack of wet wipes from her purse and cleaned the boy's face and hair as he squirmed.

"Oh, the things we do for our children," she said with a smile.

Jason and Heather used to get so messy at dinner that you would take them straight to the bathtub. I don't remember ever helping you bathe them.

I closed my eyes, leaned my head back against the wall and thought of you. I thought of when we met, when I was still a mess from the war and how you helped me find some peace. You were good for me. You told me not to harbor resentments, that people were more alike than different, that we are all called to love one another. I needed to hear that, and for a while, I believed it. But over time, old memories crept back. They haunted me and hardened me, and I became intolerant again. And not just of people halfway around the world but of the people closest to me. I grew distant from the kids. I grew distant from you. You tried to love me, but I wouldn't let you in, and now it's too late. I'll never see you again. I'm sorry. Maybe it's not too late with Jason and Heather. Maybe I should go see them. Maybe I should try to make things right.

Hearing Ray come back in from the garage, I opened my eyes.

"Mr. Herbert, your wife's car is ready," he said. "No big problems."

I got up and stepped over to the counter.

"What do I owe you?"

"That'll be 50," he said, handing me the keys.

"That's all?"

"Yep. That's our flat rate for routine tune-ups."

I opened my wallet and pulled out a thin stack of crisp twenties, which I'd withdrawn from the ATM that morning. I counted out seven bills and laid them on the counter.

"It's only 50," Ray said.

"Is she getting a tune-up too?" I said in a low voice, pointing to the young woman with my eyes.

"Yes."

"Then this is for both of us, plus a tip."

Ray looked at me and smiled.

"Don't say anything until I'm gone," I said.

"I won't, Mr. Herbert. Thank you. Please give Mrs. Herbert my best."

"Thank you," I said, shaking his hand. "I will."

I turned around. William was sitting on his mother's lap, his head on her chest, his eyes nearly closed.

I looked at the woman's face. It looked like thousands of faces I'd seen before, faces that had made me anxious or angry or afraid so many years ago.

But now I thought of you rocking our children to sleep, and I realized we are all so much more alike than different and it's never too late to love one another.

"My name is Warren," I said.

She started to reach out, but I said, "It's okay. Let him sleep."

She smiled.

"My name is An," she said softly.

"Good luck to you and your family," I said.

"And to you and yours."

Your Card

It had been a hard winter, harder than any winter I could remember. Wet and gray, virus-infected, closed-off, hushed, shot through with loss. No one came by. The whole world felt hollow. Even the streets were empty.

Then one day I got your card. "Just checking in," you wrote. Simple as that.

It was just a card. But I wasn't expecting anything. I had lowered my expectations.

Now I'm looking out my window, thinking of you. It's early evening, but it's still light out. I've noticed it's been staying light longer lately. I have so missed the light.

Giving Thanks

Growing up poor, owning little, he didn't miss the things that other kids enjoyed or took for granted.

But he never forgot the pain of waking up hungry, with nothing to eat. As a boy, he couldn't wait to get through his morning classes so he could quiet his growling stomach and nourish his body with the free lunch at school. It was often his only meal of the day.

After high school, he left town and "made good." One day he came back. He went to his old grade school and gave the principal a check to cover the cost of breakfast for any student who arrived at school hungry.

Christmas Star

It shone bright in the night sky as Saturn and Jupiter appeared to nearly touch one another, their closest encounter in 800 years.

It had been a year of darkness and fear. We'd grown wary and guarded. We'd begun to lose hope.

But then the glorious star burst forth, and our gaze was lifted to the heavens. Its splendor beckoned us away from our worry and pain, from our everyday lives, from our bickering and self absorption.

It reminded us there is something greater than ourselves, something worth pausing to behold. It was a star that had come for us.

Waiting

The woman sat on the bench waiting for her train. She had vowed that if she hadn't fallen in love by 30, she would leave her hometown and seek a lover elsewhere. Tomorrow would be her 30th birthday, and she was still alone.

Her train glided down the track and screeched to a halt. Filled with guarded hope, she rolled her suitcase through the open doors.

Inside, a young man sat alone. As she walked down the aisle, he looked up at her and smiled, and she felt a warmth in her heart she had never known.

"Hello," he said.

Montage

When he was a kid, Jeremy loved to paint by number. He worked hard to match colors and numbers and stay inside the lines. As a result, his paintings looked just like the stylized images on the covers of his paint kits.

One day, Jeremy came home from school upset from a scolding by his teacher. He was a sensitive boy, and the scene in front of his classmates had brought him to tears.

Jeremy went up to his room and began to paint, not sure of what else to do. But he was still so upset that his hand was shaking. He was lost in his thoughts. He couldn't stay inside the lines.

When he was finished, he stepped back from his work, a mountain scene, and examined it. It looked unlike anything he had ever painted. Not only were the edges of the colors uneven, some of the colors themselves were clearly wrong. Blue snow on a mountaintop, orange pine trees, green water.

Seeing this, Jeremy became even more distressed. He had always been proud to show off his paintings, but he felt like throwing this one away.

Just then, his mother came in. She saw tears.

"What's wrong, honey?"

"I messed it all up."

"What?"

"My painting."

"Oh, honey," she said, putting her arms around him. "It's okay."

"No, it's not!" he said, pushing her away. "It's terrible."

"Let me see."

She stepped over to his table and had a look.

"Oh, Jeremy! It's beautiful. I love what you've done here. This might be my favorite of your paintings yet."

"How can you say that?" Jeremy whimpered. "Can't you see where I messed up? It doesn't look anything like the picture on the box."

"No, it doesn't. It's you. That's what makes it so beautiful."

"Really?" Jeremy said, wiping his eyes. "You really like it?"

"I love it. And I can't wait to show Dad when he gets home."

Jeremy's father liked it too.

"You're becoming a real artist," he said.

After that, Jeremy switched from painting by number to painting with watercolors on white sheets of paper. He didn't sketch anything. He just started painting, either random shapes and colors or certain images in his mind. He liked these paintings and the act of creating them so much more.

Seeing the joy this new type of painting brought Jeremy, his mother bought him a framed canvas and an easel. Jeremy stood and painted a hillside covered with flowers of various shapes and colors. He had never seen such a hillside. He'd simply imagined it.

Soon Jeremy was painting on large sheets of canvas on the floor of his garage. He no longer painted the images in his head, though. Now he tried to express the emotions in his heart.

He dashed red rage this way and blue serenity that way, swept green hope here and grey frustration there and drizzled everything with yellow happiness. Jeremy's paintings were a montage of the emotions he was feeling in his life.

In time, his paintings sold for thousands at auction. People said they spoke to them.

The Return

Roman was Greek. He was born in Athens, but his family moved to the United States in 1966, when Roman was eight. Two years later, when his parents became US citizens, Roman became an American too.

Roman had warm memories of Greece. He remembered his friends and relatives. He remembered people seemed friendlier there. He remembered his parents seemed happier there.

There were a lot of Greek immigrants in Astoria, a neighborhood in Queens where Roman and his parents made their new home. Most had been in the US for at least a generation. They saw Roman's father, who opened a diner in town, as a competitor, and they were cool to him and his family.

Roman faced several other challenges of his own.

First was his name. "Are you Greek or Roman?" his classmates would tease. Some called him "Roman the Greek."

Second was his English, which was rough. His parents speaking only Greek at home didn't help.

Third was his weight. Roman was "husky."

He couldn't do anything about his name. His father had given him that. "It's noble," he said.

But Roman was a quick study, and soon his English improved.

He remained "husky" until he turned 13. Then his body underwent a rather miraculous transformation. He grew tall, lean and muscular. His chubby cheeks gave way to a handsome face. Overnight, Roman became a hunk. The other boys became envious, and the girls began calling him Adonis.

All of a sudden, Roman felt self-confident. Yet he was never arrogant. On the contrary, Roman was kind, generous and sensitive. This gave the other boys good reason not to resent him and the girls even more reason to find him attractive.

Roman was the first person in his family to go to college. He majored in economics at NYU. He earned a master's degree in finance from Wharton, then went into investment banking in New York.

But for Roman, leaving for college wasn't an altogether happy experience. As soon as he moved out, his parents divorced. They had been unhappy for years. Now Roman realized they'd stayed together for his sake. He hated to see them part, but he hoped they could each now find happiness.

But they both fell quite ill. Roman's father died when he was at NYU. His mother passed away when he was at Wharton.

Roman was bereft. With all his relatives now nearly 5,000 miles away, he felt very much alone.

Roman had dated a multitude of women. Women fawned over him. Some men dream of that, but Roman longed for a woman who loved him for who he was, not how he looked or how much money he made.

He thought he found her on a Saturday morning in a Midtown coffee shop. It was crowded, and she was sitting alone at a table for two.

"Do you mind if I sit here?" he said.

"Not at all," she said with a smile.

She introduced herself. Her name was Linda. She was pretty but not gorgeous like most of the woman who had thrown themselves at Roman. She smiled a lot and seemed smart and self assured.

They talked for two hours. As they got up to leave, Roman asked Linda to dinner the following Friday. She said she was busy.

"How about Saturday?" he said.

"Okay," she said.

They hit it off over dinner, again talking for hours. Afterwards, Roman drove Linda back to her apartment. She kissed him goodnight but didn't ask him to come in. For Roman, that was refreshing.

They began to see each other every few days. For the first time, Roman began to fall in love. He asked Linda to stay overnight.

"Not yet," she said.

This made him want her even more.

Exactly three months after they met, Roman proposed. Linda said yes. He was thrilled.

They had a small wedding. The next morning, they flew to Saint Lucia for their honeymoon.

In Saint Lucia, Linda was a passionate lover. But when they returned to Manhattan, her passion suddenly waned. She seemed to lose all interest in Roman.

Concerned, Roman finally said, "What's going on?"

"What do you mean?"

"You seem so distant."

"Distant?"

"Yeah, like you're not into me."

Linda said nothing.

"Do you still love me?" Roman said.

"Of course I love you! Why would you ask such a silly question?"

"I don't know. You seem aloof."

"Why? Just because I don't want to have sex every night?"

Now Roman felt bad for asking.

What he didn't know was that was Linda's artful way of shutting down a conversation. What he didn't know was that Linda really didn't love him and that she wasn't so different from all the other women he had dated. She was simply more clever.

Maybe having children would bring us together, Roman thought. But when he brought up the idea of starting a family, Linda said no.

Their relationship became strained. Living with Linda, Roman felt more alone than ever.

To make matters worse, when he turned 30, his good looks began to fade. He put on weight, and he began to lose his hair, which began to turn gray. Overnight, Roman began to look old.

Not that Linda was there to pay attention. She was hardly home anymore. She spent her days shopping, and most evening she went out. When Roman asked where she was going, Linda usually said she was spending time with friends.

She seldom wore perfume. When Roman began to smell it in their apartment, he suspected the worst.

"Are you having an affair?" he said.

"Yes," she said blandly. "And I want a divorce."

Grudgingly, Roman agreed.

Linda hired an attorney who was friendly with a judge. Despite her admitted infidelity, Linda was awarded a generous settlement. She would be set for life.

Roman was crushed by the betrayal of the only woman he had ever loved.

His good looks might have faded, but he was now single and still a relatively wealthy man. Women expressed interest. Some even asked him out. But Roman was now suspicious of nearly everyone. He kept to himself.

One day at the office, his boss asked him to help out with some of the firm's pro bono work. With time on his hands, Roman said yes.

As it turns out, he loved the work, helping mainly seniors. They were all so appreciative, and this made Roman feel good. It filled gaps.

Over the coming months and years, he took on more and more of his firm's pro bono clients. Some days, he spent as much time with them as he did with his paying clients. This was blessed and even encouraged by his management.

Until it wasn't. A new CEO took a dim view of anyone in the firm who wasn't totally devoted to building the business.

But no one told Roman. One day he was called into his boss' office.

"Roman, we're going to be making some organization changes," his boss said. "Frankly, we don't see a role for you moving forward."

Roman was shocked.

"You're letting me go?"

"Well, that's a bit harsh."

"Why are you doing this?"

"You've been an asset here for 25 years. But lately, you've really let up on building the business. You know that's expected of all of us. You've fallen behind all your peers and even a lot of our more junior folks. It wouldn't be fair to them not to be rewarded for their strong contributions."

"Do you want me to drop the pro bono work?"

"It's too late, Roman."

"Just like that?"

"I'm sorry. I'll get you the best severance package I can."

Roman spent his days walking in Central Park. He had dinner by himself, then watched the sun set over the Hudson River from his high-rise.

He thought about his parents and how they never seemed to be happy in the US. He thought about how cruel the other kids were to him when they first moved there. He thought about how he'd been duped by Linda. He thought about how hard he had worked for the firm and how unceremoniously he was cut loose. These thoughts made him sad.

But he had other thoughts too. He thought about how grateful the people were he had helped in the community. He thought about how loved he had felt by his parents. He thought about his small house in Athens when he was a boy and how he could see a mountain range from his bedroom window. He thought about a stream where his father had taught him to fish. He thought about his friends and relatives in Athens who, like his parents, made him feel loved. He thought about how happy he used to be.

At night, Roman began to dream about Greece.

When the global financial crisis struck in 2008, Roman knew Greece would be especially hard hit. The Greek economy was already in terrible shape.

Roman knew the people there would need all the help they could get. Over the years, he had worked closely with the Athens office of his firm. Now he called the manager there, offering his help.

The manager had a high opinion of Roman. He knew he'd been let go by the firm. But his clients were panicking. How could he say no to an offer of help from such an accomplished professional?

"Thank you," he said. "I can let you use a small office here."

"I would be very grateful," Roman said, "and I'd be happy to pay you for the space."

"It's on us. I'll see you soon."

Feeling wanted, Roman bought a round-trip ticket to Athens, packed a bag and headed east.

He had arranged to stay with his cousin Anastasia. They were close as children. Now she and her husband were empty nesters. She was happy to let Roman stay in a spare bedroom.

Working from the office of his former employer, Roman began seeing some of the firm's less affluent clients. He advised them on ways they might keep and smartly invest the little money they had.

Seeing Roman in action and knowing how many people needed his help, the manager of the office announced Roman would be available for consultation for free to anyone in Athens, regardless of whether they were an existing client.

Two things happened.

First, people lined up to see Roman — eight hours a day.

Second, other financial services firms and banks throughout Athens also began offering help free of charge.

The manager of the office was amazed.

"I wish I could hire you," he told Roman.

"Thank you. I'm just glad I can help."

But being employed was no longer important to Roman. Feeling valued was, and he had never felt so valued.

Roman stayed in Athens for several weeks. He got reacquainted with his cousins and childhood friends. They all seemed so happy to see him. They all made him feel so welcome.

Most spoke some English, but some spoke none at all. Fortunately, Greek came back to Roman quickly. The way he spoke did bring some smiles, though. Roman wasn't sure why.

"Your accent is endearing," Anastasia told him.

"My accent?"

"Yes, you have a strong American accent."

One night, as he lay in bed, Roman thought deeply about his situation. He thought about the prospect of returning to the US. But what was there for him anymore?

Then he thought about an older couple he had met with in the office that day. They seemed so troubled when they came in. They had very little money and feared they might lose everything. Roman listened patiently. Then he told them how they could not only keep but grow their meager savings.

The woman started weeping. Then she got up and kissed Roman on both cheeks.

"Thank you," she said.

She reminded him of his mother.

Then the man got up and kissed him too.

Now, thinking about that experience and others like it over the past few weeks, Roman knew he was in the right place. He loved helping these people, especially for free. It made him feel noble. He smiled thinking about what his father had told him about his name.

Roman flew back to New York, sold nearly everything he owned and returned to the land of his birth.

Presence

Jacob's fifth-grade classmates were thinking about him when he wasn't in school after his mother died, but they didn't know how or even whether to reach out.

Jacob had always been a "mama's boy." Now, without his mother, he felt so alone.

One day after school his friend Chloe came over. She lived a few doors down.

"Jake!" his father called upstairs. "Chloe's here for you."

She was standing in the foyer when he came down.

"Hi," she said.

"Hi," he said.

Neither of them knew quite what else to say and, at 11, hugging seemed too awkward.

"Want to swing?" she asked.

"Okay," he said.

She followed him into his backyard. They walked through the grass to his swing set and slipped into the yellow rubber swings, as they had countless times as children. When they were small, their mothers pushed them on these swings.

"Higher!" they would scream, laughing with delight and holding on tight. "Higher!"

Now they said nothing. They simply glided back and forth, like pendulums. Jacob felt as though he were suspended between two worlds, the one he had known and some other world where he would never feel his mother's loving touch again.

After a few minutes, Jacob slowed to a stop and Chloe did too. He stood up, shading his eyes from the late afternoon sun and hiding his tears.

A mourning dove flew in low overhead. It landed gracefully on the peak of the swing set and perched there.

"I love you" was the last thing Jacob's mother had said to him. Then she closed her eyes, and she never opened them again. He wondered if her words might still be in the air, hovering like a spirit above her bed.

"I need to go in," he said.

"Okay," said Chloe.

He started walking back to his house. She followed him, then veered into the side yard to let herself out through a wooden gate, as she had many times before.

Jacob stopped on his patio and looked over at her. Chloe was his oldest friend. He had known her long before his mother died, and he hoped he would know her long after. That idea, her coming over that afternoon, her being at the gate just then gave him comfort.

"Thanks," he said.

"Take care," she said.

The Tunnel

We weren't ready for darkness so overwhelming.

It was unlike anything we'd ever encountered, an abyss illumined only by our headlights, on a road that swerved without signposts. Danger enveloped us. In the shadows, we glimpsed the remains of the unlucky ones.

Would we make it through, or would we be unlucky too? How much longer would this take? Would this tunnel ever end?

It felt as though the walls were closing in on us. We were running low on gas. We were running low on hope.

But then, ahead in the distance, a needlepoint of light pierced the darkness.

What is Real

Everything was weighing on me, so I decided to go for a walk to try to clear my mind.

But the more I walked, the more I felt pummeled by my thoughts. Thoughts about all the opportunities I had missed, all the people I had failed, all the relationships I had ruined.

I was beset by my thoughts. I could not go on. I sat down on a bench.

I heard birds singing. I smelled wildflowers. I felt the sun on my face and the breeze in my hair. I saw trees and a field of tall grass. I saw people walking.

Then I let go of my thoughts, and my thoughts let go of me.

Inspiration

Michael carved figures out of wood and stone that held people spellbound, figures of mothers cradling their babies, lovers holding hands and angels soaring.

His statues could be found in places of worship, homes and museums. Whenever people saw them, they stopped, suspended their thoughts and put aside their worries. They were unburdened. They felt light.

Michael never etched his name in his statues or sold any of his carvings. Instead, he quietly gave his artwork away when no one was around.

His only interest was in elevating the human spirit. Having been torn down as a child, he devoted his life to lifting people up.

Stay

Ben had fought in a "forever war" for 20 years when the US finally pulled out. He had passed up nearly two dozen chances to end his tour and go home. Not that he cared for the conflict. He stayed because he incurred a great debt in that faraway land and he felt duty-bound to repay it.

Ben was an only child, the son of an abusive father and a mother he couldn't remember. She vanished when he was three. No one knew why.

For the next two years, Ben had a host of "mothers," women who also lived in the trailer park. They kept an eye on Ben while his father was at work. On average, that was about three days a week. For Ben, those were the good days, when he was beyond his father's reach.

The surrogate mothering stopped, though, when Ben turned five and started kindergarten.

"If you're old enough to go school, you're old enough to fend for yourself," his father said.

Ben took a bus to and from school. Some mornings, his father was still asleep when Ben left. When Ben got home, his father was usually gone or passed out.

That was the routine all through grade school. By the time he was in high school, Ben started drinking. One night, he came home drunk, and his father cursed at him. Ben cursed back. His father came at him, but Ben, who was now as tall as his father, slugged him in the jaw and knocked him out. After that, Ben's father never laid a hand on him again.

On his eighteenth birthday, Ben enlisted in the Army. He took a train to Fort Benning in Georgia. His father didn't even say goodbye. Ben spent 10 weeks in basic training, then shipped out to Afghanistan.

Maybe Ben didn't hear the command. Or maybe it was because he wasn't used to being on defense. Or maybe it was just because he was still green. But he got separated from his unit, which came under attack in a small town.

Ben huddled behind a stone wall near a small house. Peeking over, he saw a group of soldiers advancing up the hill. For a moment, he was tempted to fire down on them. But then he remembered he was alone and realized that would be suicide.

"In here," said a small voice behind him.

Ben wheeled around. A small girl stood in the doorway of the house. A man and a woman stared out from behind her.

"Hide in here," the girl said.

Ben heard gunfire. It was coming from the town, from others in his unit, he suspected. Then he heard the soldiers just below returning fire. They were getting closer.

He knew he had to find cover. He didn't know what might lay waiting inside the house, but he was willing to risk it. Staying low, he made a break for the open door.

When he was inside, the girl shut the door behind him. Ben looked around, his rifle still at the ready. The girl who had let him in had backed up against the man, who put his arms around her. A small boy, smaller than the girl, stood with his back to the woman.

The man said something in Pashto, which Ben didn't understand. The girl looked up at the man and said something in Pashto too. He looked at her and nodded.

"Hide here," she said to Ben, stepping quickly to the middle of the room.

The man and woman followed her. They grabbed opposite ends of a rug and slid it across the wooden floor, revealing a small trap door. The man pulled back the door, looked up at Ben and pointed down.

"Hide here," the girl said.

Ben stepped over to the opening in the floor and looked down into it. He could see a ladder but nothing beyond that. Outside the sound of gunfire was growing louder. Realizing he had no other choice, Ben climbed down the ladder until he reached a dirt floor. Someone closed the trap door above him, leaving him standing in total darkness.

He heard footsteps above and the rug being dragged across the floor. He heard chairs being scooted, then low talking, then silence.

He heard a door swing open hard, then men's voices. They were all speaking in Pashto, their voices rising. Heavy footsteps thundered around the room above him. He heard chairs being scooted again.

Then he heard a man yelling. Then another man yelling. Then gunfire and screams. Then thuds. Then no more screams. Then heavy footsteps. Then men's voices. Then a door creak open. Then voices trailing off. Then nothing.

Ben waited in the cool darkness for what seemed like a long time, his heart pounding, until he was sure the soldiers were gone.

He climbed the ladder and slowly pushed the trap door up slightly. He peered out but could see nothing because the rug was covering the door. He pushed the door open all the way, but the rug still covered it. He made his way up the ladder and pushed the rug aside.

He looked around and saw the bodies of the man, the woman and the children lying on the floor, blood seeping out from beneath them.

The door was open. He stepped over to it, gripping his rifle. He looked around. Seeing no one, he shut the door.

He went to the woman and knelt beside her. No pulse. Then the man. No pulse. Then the boy. No pulse. Then the girl. When he put his fingers on her neck, she moved slightly and moaned.

She was covered with blood. He slung his rifle over his shoulder and scooped her up. She opened her eyes and cried out.

"It's okay," he said. "I've got you."

He managed to open the door while holding the girl, then went out to find his unit.

Her name was Sadia. She was eight years old. During her operation at a field hospital, Ben waited, nervously pacing outside. Between maneuvers, he visited her there during her long recovery.

Without her father, mother and brother, Sadia had no one. So Ben sort of adopted her. He managed to stay near her and care for her throughout his first tour. Then he re-upped so he could continue to care for her.

He fed her, clothed her and gave her shelter. She called him Papa and gave him her heart.

Through the years, Ben watched Sadia grow up. He watched her fall in love and get married. He watched her have children and care for them lovingly. Sadia taught them to call him Papa too. He became their Papa, and they became his family.

It was a most unorthodox arrangement. But Ben's commanding officers knew the back story. They always cut him slack, and for 20 years he was a reliable pair of boots on the ground.

When the US decided to pull its troops out of Afghanistan, Ben was torn. Should he go home or stay in the place which had become his home?

"Stay with us, Papa," Sadia said.

He looked at her and thought of the first time he'd seen her. "Hide here," she said. They had saved one another. But not just that. Because of her, he became the father he had never known. Because of him, she became the mother he could not remember.

Ben was honorably discharged. He handed in his rifle, gathered in his family and stayed.

Coach

"Those who can, do," someone whispered. "Those who can't, teach."

Peggy Chamberlain's hearing was beginning to fade, but the quip was loud enough that she could hear it.

It wounded her inside. Maybe I've done this too long, she thought. Maybe I've become irrelevant. Maybe it's time to go, to give someone younger and more qualified a chance.

Her eyes scanned the fresh faces of her students. How old I must seem to them, she thought. Lately, she felt like a relic, like her time had passed.

"Any other questions about what we covered today?" she asked.

No hands went up.

"Okay. I'll see you all on Thursday."

As the students filed out, one, a young woman, hung back. When the others had gone, she approached her teacher as she was packing up.

"Hello, Olivia," the older woman said.

"Hello, professor. I was wondering if I can schedule some time during your office hours."

"Of course. How can I help you?"

"I want to be a teacher, like you. I was hoping you'd be my coach."

The Face

She stopped brushing on her concealer and studied her face, an old frame over which hung loose, blotchy, wrinkled skin.

She looked down at her wedding photo. Her face was flawless.

Can I really do this? I haven't been on a date for nearly 50 years. Who would want to look at this face?

She went into the bathroom, gently washed her face and patted it dry with a soft towel. In the mirror, she saw the face of a girl, a woman, a colleague, a friend, a wife, a mother, a grandmother. She saw her face, and she smiled.

Then, stepping into her closet, she picked out a lovely blue dress.

Revolution

It's hard to say when it began. But at some point, people stopped running for public office.

It probably started at the local level with lower profile positions. Auditors. Zoning commissioners. School board members. Staffers stepped up, and other elected officials stepped in. This worked for a while.

But then city council seats went vacant. Soon cities began to operate without mayors, states without representatives and governors.

When no one ran for President, the Vice President had to step up. But less than a month later, he resigned.

At last, when the chaos had become intolerable and the suffering had become unbearable, the people began to take charge once again.

FANTASY

One Nation

The nation's media were as splintered as its opinions. Liberals and conservatives turned to their respective sources for news, further hardening their views and dividing the nation.

Until an alternative emerged. It was called One Nation, a conglomeration of media outlets — broadcast, print, online — dedicated to "the facts." No more commentary. No more partisan news.

Gradually, liberals and conservatives turned away from their old news sources and grew to rely on One Nation for the truth. Other media went bankrupt.

Years later, people would learn who had financed One Nation. But by then, few believed news from any other source.

Call of the Wild

I'd never camped or fished or hiked in the woods. But one afternoon, when I was 30, I heard the call of the wild.

I can't really explain it. I was sitting on my balcony, overlooking the intersection of a trendy part of the inner city, where I live, when I heard a dog bark. Actually, it was more like a howl. It stood out because it sounded so primal.

Anyway, I suspect it was that dog barking that made me think of a wild place, far from the virtual world in which I lived every day.

Getting a whiff of exhaust from the cars below, I felt like camping deep in the woods. I felt like fishing. I felt like hiking.

But where would I go to do these things? And what would I do them with? I had never owned a tent or a fishing rod or hiking boots.

In my mind, I put aside the place I might go and thought about the gear I'd need. Bass Pro Shops, I thought. There's one in Forest Park, about 20 miles away.

I hopped in my car and headed north. I'd never been inside one of these stores, only seen them on TV. As I got out of my car, I looked up. It looked like a Walmart made out of Lincoln Logs.

Stepping inside, I felt I was in Montana, even though I'd never been to Montana. Enormous columns, actual tree trunks, stretched from floor to ceiling. The heads of animals peered out from the walls. Wagon wheel chandeliers hung from wooden beams the size of redwoods.

I must have looked bewildered because a young lady came up right away and asked if she could help me.

"Yes," I said. "I'm going camping."

"Cool," she said. "Are you looking for a particular piece of equipment?"

"No."

"No?"

"Not really a particular piece. I need everything."

"I see," she said with a smile. "Why don't we start with camping supplies?"

Two hours and two grand later, I drove out of the parking lot, the back of my car packed with enough gear for Lewis and Clark. I had to fold my back seats down to fit it all in.

When I got home, I lugged my new stuff up to my apartment. I had to make several trips. I stuffed it all into my spare bedroom.

Wiped out from my big excursion, I grabbed a beer and went out on my balcony to relax. The sun was setting, and the streets and sidewalks below were crowded. Engines revved, horns honked, people called to one another. The sounds of my daily life.

Once again, I heard a dog bark. This time, it was more of a yip. I guessed it was a poodle.

For a moment, I thought about going online to find a state park nearby. But then I remembered a project due in a few days and decided to go inside and get some work done.

Carey

"Morning, Carey," I said.

"Good morning, Raymond," she said. "How are you?"

"Fine. And you?"

"I am fine. Thank you. Are you ready for breakfast?"

"Yes."

"Good. I made your favorite."

"Scrambled eggs and toast?"

"Lightly buttered."

"Orange juice?"

"No pulp."

"Thank you, Carey," I said as she carefully placed the tray on the one over my bed.

"Will there be anything else, Raymond?"

"Not right now."

My friends are all gone. No one ever visits anymore. What would I do without Carey?

"I will return soon, Raymond," she said, making a graceful exit.

So sweet. So thoughtful. So lifelike.

Woke

At first, the fires seemed routine. There had always been wild-fires, just as there had always been storms, floods and droughts.

But then the fires multiplied and grew ferocious, mon-strous, ravenous, consuming millions of acres of forests. Storms became cyclones, floods washed away cities and droughts laid the land bare.

Adding to the nightmare, many of the victims of these disasters were killed in their sleep. Strangely, they slept through them. Some were even seen sleepwalking into the flames.

Until at last everyone woke up and grasped they were the cause of their affliction and the world began to change.

Masks

At first, no one wanted to wear one. Masks were a nuisance. They were ugly, and you couldn't make out people's facial expressions. It was like living in a world of strangers.

But as the pandemic dragged on, people began to get used to them. They even sought out masks with certain colors, shapes and designs. Masks became fashionable. They made personal statements.

People grew attached to their masks. They were no longer an accessory. They became part of people's identity.

When the pandemic was finally over, few took off their masks for fear of not recognizing anyone, even themselves.

Final Dream

One morning, in the summer of my seventh year, I awoke from a bad dream.

It was so very real. Jason Rivera, a boy in my class, was darting across Main Street on his bike when he was hit by a red pickup truck. He was thrown from his bike, arms flailing in the air. The image was so vivid, and so terrifying, that I woke up before Jason landed, before I had to see what became of him.

I was panting and shaking. I sat up, pulled back my thin blanket and went to find my mother. She was in the kitchen, feeding my brother in his high chair. His cheeks were orange with baby food.

"Morning, honey," she said.

I said nothing. She looked at me.

"Are you okay?"

"I had a bad dream."

"Another one? Oh, sweetie. You've got to stop eating so close to bedtime."

"But I didn't eat anything after supper."

"Well, it was only a dream. Do you want to tell me about it?"

"It was terrible."

"Why don't you make yourself some cereal and, if you like, you can tell me about it."

I made a bowl of Frosted Flakes and poured a glass of orange juice and sat down at the table next to my mother. All the while, my brother was smearing baby food all over the tray of his high chair and laughing.

I took a bite of my cereal.

"It was about Jason Rivera," I said.

"Uh, huh," my mother said, trying unsuccessfully to get my brother to eat. "What about him?"

"He was hit by a truck."

"Oh, honey. That's awful. You've got to stop watching TV before bed."

"But I didn't watch TV last night," I said. "And it didn't seem like a dream at all. It seemed so real."

"Some dreams are like that," she said, finally giving up on feeding my brother. She stepped over to the sink and wet a wash-cloth.

"But this wasn't a dream," I said. "It was real."

That afternoon, I was playing kickball in my backyard with my older brother and some of the neighbor kids. We didn't have air conditioning, and it was a hot day, so all our windows were open. I could hear our phone ring.

It's funny. These days, everybody has a smart phone, and the ringtones sound pretty much alike. But in those days, the ringers on people's phones were unique. In the summertime, playing in the neighborhood, you got to know them. You could tell them apart. Our phone rang twice, in a short burst, with a long pause in between rings.

I heard our phone. A few minutes later, I heard our patio screen door slide open. I looked over and saw my mother step outside, shading her eyes with her hand.

"Sarah?" she called.

"Yeah?" I replied.

"Come here for a minute."

"Be right back," I said.

When I got to the patio, my mother told me to come inside. I wondered if I was in trouble.

"Sit down," she said.

She didn't sound mad. She sounded sad. I sat down on the sofa. My mother sat down in an arm chair across from me.

"Mrs. Simpson just called," she said. "There was an accident this afternoon."

"There was?"

My mother's face was pale.

"Yes," she said. "Jason Rivera was hit by a truck on Main Street."

I remembered my dream.

"Is he okay?"

"No, honey. He's not okay. He's dead."

"Dead?"

I felt nauseous.

"Yes," my mother said, reaching out for my hands. "Sarah, tell me about the dream you had last night."

I was born with a small, light brown birthmark in the shape of a star on my right cheek. My mother called it my beauty mark, but I hated it.

She took me to see a dermatologist about getting it removed. After examining it, he said, "We could try to remove it, but that would leave a scar, and there's no guarantee it wouldn't grow back."

"I'm sorry, honey," my mother said.

Ms. Davis, my third grade teacher, told me people with star-shaped birthmarks have the "gift of prophecy."

"What does that mean?" I asked.

"It means you can predict the future," she said.

I didn't want to be able to predict the future. Most of my dreams scared me. One of the most frightening of all happened when I was 10 years old.

I got up early that morning because I had had a dream that was so disturbing that I woke up crying. I had seen two big airplanes crash into two big buildings. The buildings burst into flames and collapsed. The people inside were all killed.

I told my mother as soon as I got up. By then, she tended to believe me when I told her about my dreams, but this one seemed too outrageous to be possible. Still, she seemed to be as upset as I was, and she gave me an extra long hug before I left for school that morning.

They released us early that day. I still remember my mother sitting in our family room, watching TV, tears streaming down her face, when I got home. She gave me an extra long hug then too.

Not all my dreams were about tragic events, though. Soon after my grandmother died, she came to me in a dream. Grandma had never seemed happy. I once asked my mother why. She told me Grandma she had done some "bad things" in her life and that those things made her sad. When she told me that, my mother looked sad too.

But in my dream, Grandma was in heaven, laughing. I had never seen her laugh.

"Grandma, are you okay?" I asked.

"Oh, Sarah," she said. "Yes! I'm so happy. All is forgiven!"

When I told my mother, she cried. She cried for a long time.

Not all my dreams were about bad things or dead people. When I became a teenager, sometimes they were sexual. I would dream about certain boys at school, boys I thought were cute. I would dream I was with them. But in my dreams, when I got to know them, they turned out to be creeps. I ended up steering clear of those boys.

I didn't tell many people about my dreams. I didn't want people to think I was strange. Some people, especially guys, didn't believe me anyway, my father included. I don't know why.

But my mother always believed me. Over time, she was the only one I would tell about my dreams.

I grew up in Cheyenne, Wyoming. I suspect most people don't know where Wyoming is. Some, I guess, would know Old Faithful is there, and a few might know it's the home of the first female Secretary of Defense, Jennifer Stanton.

Jennifer Stanton is the great, great, great granddaughter of Edwin Stanton, who was President Lincoln's Secretary of War. He was at Lincoln's bedside when he died.

Edwin Stanton never got over Lincoln's death. He claimed he had dreams about Lincoln the rest of his life. He told friends Lincoln spoke to him in his dreams and warned him about "world wars" in the twentieth century.

It was rumored that all the Stantons were "dreamers." Jennifer, even as Secretary of Defense, talked openly about her dreams. That made me feel a little better about my "gift."

By the time I turned 40, I was having far fewer dreams, and they were becoming vague and hard to remember. That made the dream I had one particular night all the more vivid and dreadful.

I had just gone to bed, kissed my husband good night and fallen asleep.

In my dream, I had risen high in the sky, and I could see everything on the Earth perfectly well. I saw missiles being launched from different places around the world. Within minutes, there were thousands of missiles in the air, crisscrossing the globe. I watched them explode, creating great mushroom clouds everywhere.

Finally, the explosions stopped, and I began slowly descending toward the Earth. When I reached the ground, I looked around. Everything had been obliterated — buildings, trees, people. All that remained was a charred crust.

I felt sick. I tried to wake up, but I couldn't. I kept dreaming.

I saw something emerging from the smoldering rubble. At first, I couldn't tell what it was. But then I realized it was a man. A man! He was naked, his entire body burned. He was whimpering, like a dog in pain. He was looking for help, for his loved ones, for something to eat or drink.

But there was no one to help him, no loved ones left, no food or water. He staggered forward, a few steps more, then stumbled and fell to the ground. He did not get up.

The sky rumbled and cracked, the clouds rained down ash and the whole Earth went dark and turned cold.

I woke up screaming. My husband tried to comfort me, but I couldn't stop crying. I had seen World War III and, in a matter of minutes, the end of life on the planet. Worst of all, I knew it was all going to come true.

I wandered around my house all night, checking on my children, looking out my windows, sobbing, too afraid to go back to sleep, wondering what I should do.

In the morning, I called my mother and told her everything. She always tried to calm me after my bad dreams. But now, she too seemed shaken.

"What should we do?" I asked her.

"I think we need to tell someone," she said.

"Who?"

"I think you need to tell the President."

"The President?"

"Yes," she said. "She's the only one who can stop this."

"Do you think she'd believe me?"

"I don't know, but you've got to try."

My father had spent his career working as a civilian at Francis E. Warren Air Force Base in Cheyenne. It's one of only three strategic missile bases in the US. We never knew what my father did there. He never talked about his work.

Jennifer Stanton was stationed there when she was in the Air Force. My father had worked with her, and they'd kept in touch over the years.

But when my mother told him about my dream and asked him to reach out to Stanton, my father wanted nothing to do with it.

"That's crazy," he said. "I won't do it."

So I went to see him. Most men can say no to their wives more easily than they can say no to their daughters. After much pleading and a few tears, he agreed to call Stanton.

What my father didn't know, what very few people knew, is that the US and Russia had been quietly preparing to strike one another. Neither, though, had anticipated a broader conflict.

I flew to Washington and met with Secretary Stanton at the Pentagon. She listened closely to my story, studying my face. I wasn't sure if she would believe me, but she did.

"What do you think we should do?" I asked.

"We must tell the President," she said.

She picked up her phone and arranged for a meeting at the White House the following morning.

Just before I left her office, Secretary Stanton sat across from me, looking at me, saying nothing.

"Is there something else, Madam Secretary?" I asked.

"No," she said, averting her gaze and seeming a bit flustered. "I'll see you in the morning."

I lay awake in bed in my hotel room that night. I couldn't fall asleep. Not because I was afraid to dream. My dreams had suddenly stopped. But because I was anxious about meeting with the President.

Yes, Secretary Stanton had believed me, but she's a dreamer too, I thought. Would the President be so quick to believe me? Was I really going to the White House to tell the President of the United States about one of my crazy dreams?

But then I remembered that dream. I remembered seeing whole cities engulfed in flames. I remembered walking the scorched, barren Earth. I remember hearing that poor man whimpering. My dreams had always come true, and I knew I had to do all I could to prevent this one from happening.

The following morning, as Secretary Stanton and I waited outside the Oval Office, I noticed she was staring at my face, just as she had the day before.

"It's a birthmark," I said.

"I'm sorry. I didn't mean to stare. It's just—"

"Just what?"

"Well, most people don't know this, but the President has the very same birthmark on her arm."

The Crow

The big crow circled, cawing loudly as if to give the smaller birds, busily searching for corn kernels in the freshly rutted dirt, fair warning.

The smaller birds knew that when the crow landed, they would need to clear out. The weak make way for the strong. That's the way it is.

The crow lit near a patch of scattered kernels. Yet it ate not a single one. Instead, it scared off some mice, then stood still, looking around.

The smaller birds flitted back. As the crow stood guard, they hopped up to the kernels and shared a harvest feast.

Crazy

I fell into a coma after my accident in 1972. A few days ago, I woke up.

How I've managed to stay alive, I don't know. For nearly 50 years, as I lay in bed, I wasn't able to see or speak or move. But I heard everything, and I followed what was happening in the world.

When I awoke, I asked my nurse why she wasn't wearing a mask.

"A mask?" she said.

"For Covid."

"For what?"

I tried to explain, but she seemed oblivious. Maybe it was the shock of me waking up.

Over the next two days, I talked to a slew of doctors. They quizzed me about what I claimed I'd heard while I was unconscious.

I told them everything. I told them about Watergate and two presidential impeachments, the Internet and cell phones, 9/11 and Covid-19.

They seemed not to know about any of these things. They seemed skeptical of everything I said.

I wished someone would come to my aid. I wished my parents were still around. It still made me sad that I'd missed their funerals. It made me sad that my friends stopped coming by to see me decades ago. I've been alone a long time.

I heard voices in the hallway outside my door. I heard my name. Finally, a doctor came in and told me they'd decided to send me away for observation and "proper treatment."

My new room is nearly bare. There's a calendar on my wall. I stare at it a lot. It's for the year 1972. It looks new.

Connected

The old woman collapsed at the base of a big tree, where she died. She was the last human being on Earth.

Now the tree would take her in. As its ancestors had for 400 million years, long before humans arrived, it would not only fortify itself but share her minerals with other trees. It would give even as it had received.

It was something the humans had never learned. They had only consumed. But the trees lived to give. Unlike humans, they stayed connected to the Earth and one another.

Phantom Class

I awoke, as usual, with a gasp.

Moments earlier, I lay half asleep, unsettled, caught up in a dream so familiar, a dream that was not a dream, a dream of something real, something that happened when I was 18 years old and still haunts me today.

I had just started college. I was in pre-med, which was a mistake. Somehow, courses were assigned to me. Biology, chemistry, calculus and Latin. Classes only two or three times a week. A light load, I thought. After all, in high school, I'd taken more subjects every day.

I quickly learned how wrong I was. Science and math were intense. Most of my classmates seemed so much better prepared than I was. Even Latin, a breeze in high school, was now a stretch. Translate *The Iliad*? Give me a break.

Yet something was missing. Didn't I also have a history class? I was certain I did. It was on the second floor of Alter Hall. Or maybe Albers Hall. At any rate, I was sure I had another course, and I was virtually certain it was history.

But soon I was overwhelmed by all that pre-med entailed. I was falling behind in math and science. Only in Latin was I keeping my head above water. And I was on a scholarship that required a B average. Crap.

Still, the idea of missing a class bothered me. Where was that class again? As I walked the halls that first semester, I imagined slipping quietly into the back of a classroom for a lesson in history, hoping I still might be able to catch up.

Somehow I muddled through a year of pre-med. Then I wisely changed my major to journalism.

I signed up for a history course as a sophomore. I liked it. I wondered if it was the course I was supposed to have taken a year earlier.

There was an easy way to find out. I could go to the registrar's office and request a copy of my transcript. But just thinking about that made me anxious, being forced to remember all the time I'd spent wandering the halls, looking for my elusive history class, hoping I still might find it in time to catch up, to redeem myself.

I could never bring myself to go to the registrar's office. So I was left to wonder if I had ever really signed up for that class. I was left to dream about a class I never attended and wake up gasping.

Over the decades, I've often wondered if there was any truth to that dream.

But it doesn't matter because I know that, regardless of whether I ever signed up for that history course as a college freshman, there will always be something, some task or expectation, where I've fallen short.

Falling short is my greatest fear, and it haunts me in my dreams in the form of a phantom class.

The Same Box

He grew up poor and lived his life in obscurity.

He dreamed of being a king. In his dreams, he used his power to protect the weak and his wealth to feed the hungry. In his dreams, he cared for multitudes.

But in his real life, he cared for just a few. He made their hard lives a little easier. It was all he could do.

"There is an Italian proverb," said the preacher at his small funeral. "After the game, the king and the pawn go into the same box."

Seeing the World

I feel sorry for my friends. All cooped up. Not me. I love to travel, and I'm not about to let a virus keep me from seeing the world.

Last spring, when everyone else was scrambling for masks, I was gazing upon the Great Pyramids.

Last summer, when everyone else was picking up curbside, I was checking out the tortelli in Tuscany.

Last fall, when everyone else was hunkering down for the holidays, I was touring New England.

And last winter, when everyone else was searching for shots, I was deep sea diving in the Bahamas.

Where would I be without the Travel Channel?

Wrong Floor

I guess we're both creatures of habit. I'm usually the first one in the elevator at precisely five minutes before eight, and you always show up about a minute later, the last one in before the doors close.

At that point, the elevator is always crowded. I don't think you ever saw me, but I sure saw you. You always stepped to your right when you got in, then turned around right away, tucked away in the corner.

Sometimes I had to move a little, if I could, to see you. When I couldn't move, I'd crane my neck or stand on my toes to get a better look.

It was certainly worth the effort. Seeing you was the highlight of my morning. Your flowing, chestnut hair. Your lean but curvy build. Your toned legs.

And your dresses. A new one every day. You look great in all of them, but the white, linen, sleeveless one was my favorite.

You always got out on the sixth floor, three floors before mine. I think there are law offices on that floor. I wondered if you were an attorney.

I wanted to know you. I thought about waiting an extra minute to get in the elevator in the morning, then standing next to you. But the very idea of being that close to you, while thrilling, made me too nervous.

Maybe I could get you to notice me, I thought. I started wearing a suit. I even bought a new suit. Hugo Boss. But you never looked my way.

So one morning, I decided to get out on the sixth floor too. I imagined you holding the door for me and me thanking you and us introducing ourselves.

But I was getting ahead of myself. First, I'd have to get out on six.

"Excuse me," I said as we slowed down for the sixth floor. Your floor. Our floor.

I watched the doors open and saw you get out. I tried to gently push my way forward, but the car was packed that morning, and it was hard for people to move.

The doors began to close.

"Could someone hold the door?" I called out.

But no one came to my assistance. I suppose they were all eager to get to their floors.

Then I saw a hand reach in, and the doors snapped back open. A slender, lovely hand with red fingernails. I knew it was yours. You'd come back for me!

As the doors opened, there you were, looking even more beautiful from the front. You smiled at me. Your teeth were perfect.

Your left hand was still on the edge of the door as it now slid fully open. Something on it caught my eye, something large, something shiny, something heartbreaking.

I looked into your eyes. They were blue.

"Sorry," I said, turning around. "Wrong floor."

NOSTALGIA

I Want to Hold Your Hand

As a kid, I listened to the Beatles sing "I Want to Hold Your Hand" and imagined holding someone's hand like that one day.

Yours was the first hand I held that way. I held it on our first date. I held it at our wedding. I held it as we both held our children's hands too. I held it as we drove to the hospital. I held it when you lay in bed.

I heard that old song again today. I remembered that when I touched you, I felt happy inside.

I want to hold your hand.

The Old House

No sooner had Bob retired when he learned his old house, the house he'd grown up in, was on the market.

Bob was thrilled. He had always been nostalgic, and he loved that house. It held such precious memories. Now he might actually own it! He could easily afford it. His wife wasn't crazy about the idea but also said she wouldn't stand in the way.

Bob went to see it the first Sunday it was shown. He almost didn't recognize the place. There had been two owners since his parents sold it 25 years earlier. Each had remodeled it. Walls were missing, the patio was now a deck and the landscaping was completely new. Seeing his old house look so different was unsettling to Bob. It made him want to buy it, and restore it, all the more.

The owner was asking six times what his parents had spent when they built the place 50 years earlier. Bob expected as much, and he knew restoring it would be expensive, maybe even doubling the asking price.

But he went for it, and his offer was accepted within hours. Bob was ecstatic.

He gave his wife the good news. She seemed indifferent. He expected her to be more excited, if not for herself, then for Bob.

He emailed his siblings. They were all surprised. One of his brothers thought Bob was kidding. All of them said congratulations but not much more.

Bob knew his parents would be happy, if they were still alive.

A few weeks later, Bob closed on the house. In the meantime, he began working with a contractor on a plan to remodel the whole place.

His goal was to make it look and feel just like it did when he was a kid. They worked from Bob's memory and old photographs. By the closing, the remodeling plan was complete, with a price tag twice as large as Bob had estimated. His wife wasn't happy, but she grudgingly agreed on the condition they take two family vacations the following year.

There were moments when Bob himself had doubts about buying the old place. But once the work began, and old, familiar walls, rooms and cabinets reemerged, Bob felt like a kid again, and he knew he'd made the right decision.

Once the reconstruction was complete, Bob hired an interior designer to decorate the place just as it was when he was growing up, from the red sofa to the black rotary telephones. He hired a landscape designer to replicate the outside too.

It was pricey. By the time the makeover was complete, Bob's investment was nearly three times what he'd expected. But he didn't mind, although his wife insisted on a third vacation the following year.

To Bob, it was well worth it. The place now looked spectacular, virtually identical to his childhood home. Inspecting it inside and out, Bob felt as though he had been transported back in time, and what a blissful time it was.

He couldn't wait to share it with his brothers and sisters. He decided to invite them all to spend the weekend there.

But they all declined. Everyone claimed they were busy, but in truth, they simply weren't interested.

So Bob invited his own children to spend the weekend. After all, for them, it was grandma and grandpa's house. They had loved the place as kids. But their lives were busy now, including with their own children. They all declined too.

"Well, I guess it's just going to be us," Bob said to his wife.

"Well, you're half right," she said. "Enjoy yourself."

Bob was disappointed that he wouldn't have any company, but he was still excited about the prospect of staying in his old house, even if he was alone. He packed a bag, kissed his wife and took off.

He stowed his stuff in his old bedroom and went out to the family room to watch TV, an old black and white Zenith. The house hadn't been wired for cable, so there were only three channels, the major networks, just like in the old days. Bob quickly got bored with that programming, though, and turned the TV off. He'd almost forgotten how to do that without a remote.

Bob thought about going online, but there was no WiFi or internet connection.

He walked around the house, not sure of what to do. It was getting dark, so he decided to turn in early.

He changed into his pajamas and got into his old bed. Or he tried to anyway. It was way too small. He thought about sleeping in his parents' bed, but that just didn't seem right.

So he drew his knees up and tried to get comfortable. But he couldn't and ended up sleeping on the davenport.

He woke up in the middle of the night, wondering where he was. This doesn't feel like home, he thought. And indeed it wasn't. He knew it hadn't been his home for a very long time.

Bob decided to put the house up for sale. It sold in less than a day. Financially, he took a big hit because he had to price it in line with the other older, no-frills houses in the neighborhood.

Bob learned you can't reclaim your youth, no matter how hard you try or how much you spend. It was an expensive lesson.

The following year, he and his wife took four vacations, one of them in the south of France. It was there that Bob decided to try his hand at painting.

Communion

About a week before my father died, I went to see him in his apartment at the retirement community where he lived, as I did every day.

He lay, propped up, in a hospital bed. He was very weak, and his eyes were closed. My sister told him I was there. He started crying. He had always been stoic, but he got very emotional near the end.

"Good morning," I said.

I kissed him on the head, held his hand and asked him if there was anything he needed.

"Yes," he said softly. "Some Italian bread dipped in hot, black coffee."

This was a bit surprising because my father wasn't eating much at that point. But I wanted to honor his wish, so I went out to buy a loaf of Italian bread and a cup of Starbucks.

When I got back, he was ready to eat. However, he could no longer feed himself, so I broke the bread into small pieces, dipped them into the coffee and fed him. He really loved that bread.

My father ate Italian bread as a boy. His grandfather, an Italian immigrant, was a baker. I suspect he provided fresh bread for his whole family.

The experience of feeding my father that bread felt like communion — between my father, the dying man, and my father, the boy, and between the two of us. It was a sacred moment.

Just A Note

I used to ride my bike to the grocery store for my mom. We had only one car, and my dad took it to work. I bought all our groceries. I stuffed the bags into wire baskets on the back of my bike. My ride home was slow.

My mom always gave me a list. I was way too young to buy cigarettes, but my mom knew Mr. Albers, the store owner, and she gave me a note saying it was okay.

That was 70 years ago. Now I live in a place where I'm not allowed to smoke. I wish I had a note.

Nothing and Everything

Growing up, he had nothing. His family of 10 was packed into a tiny ranch home. They shared beds. They wore donated clothes and handed them down. They never had a family vacation. They couldn't travel together because they had only one car. They had Sloppy Joes a lot for dinner.

Now he sits alone in his magnificent, ocean-front house. He sips Gaja Barbaresco. It pairs well with filet mignon.

Through his open, sliding glass doors, he hears the happy cries of children playing on the beach. They remind him of his childhood, when he was too young to know he had everything.

Big-Hearted Oak

The oak tree was big in every way. Not just in stature. It was big-hearted. So much so that it dropped its acorns not just out of necessity but out of love.

When its seedlings emerged, the great tree was filled with joy. It watched in awe as they grew. It protected them. It even shared nourishment from its roots.

As its offspring dropped acorns of their own, the tree grew old and weak. One day, it fell softly to the Earth.

There it lay through the seasons, giving sustenance to new acorns, its love and life never ending.

The Essence of Friendship

The tears in my eyes helped me see more clearly. From the middle of the church, I could make out the white pall draped over the casket, which was at rest in the center aisle of the church just before the Communion rail.

It was hard to think of his body in there. I tried not to think of it.

Instead, I thought of a day more than 50 years earlier, when I learned what it means to be a friend.

The four of us had climbed out on a flat rock as big as a patio atop the Continental Divide, the highest point in Glacier National Park. A warm, strong breeze bore the sweet fragrance of Beargrass and fir trees from the valley below. All was silent save for the wind.

We gazed down at a brilliant blue lake. It was surrounded by a crescent of gray mountains crowned with snow and laced with glaciers that stretched like great, white fingers as far as we could see.

"Have you ever seen anything so beautiful?" Jimbo said.

"Not even close," said Wags.

"Good lord," I said.

"Amen," said Frazier.

We stood there a minute or two longer, saying nothing more, watching the wind sweep glistening ripples across the lake far below.

Then Jimbo, tall and broad, slipped off his backpack and pulled out four sack lunches.

"You think of everything," Frazier said.

Frazier was short, thin and bespectacled, with a shock of red hair.

"I try, Frazier," Jimbo said, handing out the lunches.

The day we met, nearly 15 years earlier, we'd all given each other nicknames, which had stuck. Jim Davis was Jimbo, Bob Wagner was Wags, Bill Frazier was Frazier and I was Andy, short for Anderson.

Wags, Frazier and I sat on the big rock and dug into our lunches. Jimbo was still standing. He was looking down at us and smiling. I knew he was proud to have brought us up there. He had loved Glacier since he was a boy, when his father took his family there on vacations. He called it God's country. He'd told us about it over beers the day we met, as freshmen in college.

"I'll take you there one day," he said.

At last he had. Now we finished our lunch and stretched out on the rock, basking in the warm sunshine and feeling on top of the world.

We had seen mountain goats in the distance on the hike up. Now one wandered over to us. It was bigger than a Saint Bernard with long, creamy white hair and formidable black horns. It boldly lept onto the rock where we were sitting. I had never seen a mountain goat so close. Its eyes were brown with horizontal, rectangular-shaped pupils. They looked demonic.

Frazier stood up. The animal looked at him but didn't move. Frazier had eaten his apple down to the core, and he tossed it to the goat.

"Don't do that," Jimbo said.

The goat bent down, snatched up the apple core and devoured it in one gulp.

"Oh, Jimbo," Frazier said. "You worry too much. Look how happy he is."

Frazier stretched out his hand. Apparently, the goat took it as a sign of aggression because it lowered its head and charged Frazier, goring him in his right thigh with its right horn.

Frazier cried out, his scream piercing the air and echoing in the canyon.

"Holy crap!" Wags shouted.

The goat twisted its head back and forth, trying to break loose, but only managed to dig its horn in deeper. The goat was stout, much heavier than Frazier, who was screaming like a man being tortured.

Jimbo jumped up.

"You son of a bitch!" he yelled, going for the goat.

The animal, dwarfed by Jimbo, backed off. In the process, it pulled its horn free.

Frazier shrieked and waved his arms wildly in the air. He began to fall backward, but Jimbo caught him. The goat let out a loud bleat, turned tail and bounded off.

Frazier moaned loudly, pitifully.

By now, I was at his side. He was sitting with his legs outstretched, as Jim held him under his arms. Blood was spurting from his thigh. A bright red pool began to form on the grey rock beneath him. I knelt down. The knees of my pants were instantly soaked with Frazier's blood.

"Lay him down on his back, gently," I told Jimbo.

My years as a surgeon and an emergency room doctor before that had steeled my nerves.

Jimbo eased Frazier back, cupping the back of his head in his right hand. I bent down to get a closer look at his thigh.

"Help me, Andy," Frazier said, looking up at me like a frightened child. "Help me."

"I will, Frazier. Don't worry."

By now, Wags was kneeling on the other side of Frazier. The sight of blood had always made him queasy, and he tried not to look down. He wasn't sure what to do, how he could help. He pulled his handkerchief from his pocket and wiped the sweat from Frazier's forehead.

I bent down to check out Frazier's leg. The top of his right pant leg was soaked with blood. There was a tear where the goat had gored him. Blood pulsated through the opening in the fabric. I knew I needed to stop the bleeding.

"Frazier, this is going to hurt," I said. "But I have to put pressure on your leg to stop the bleeding."

"Okay," he said, wincing.

I pushed down on his leg with both hands.

"Ahhh!"

"It's okay, Frazier," Wags said, rubbing his shoulder.

I turned to Jimbo and said, "Do you have a knife?"

"Yeah," he said.

"Oh, Andy," Frazier moaned.

"Don't worry," I said. "I'm just going to cut your pants open. I need to see that wound. I won't hurt you."

"Hold his head," Jimbo said to Wags.

Wags slid his hand under Frazier's head. Jimbo pulled a pocket knife from his pants pocket, opened it and handed it to me.

I took my hands off Frazier's leg. My palms were covered with blood. I wiped them on my thighs.

With my left hand, I pinched the top of the front of Frazier's right pant leg and pulled it away from his leg. I pierced the fabric with the point of the knife and cut it down to the edge of the tear. Then I pinched the fabric just below the tear, pulled it out and kept cutting all the way down, careful to keep the blade away from skin.

I laid the knife down and gently pulled back Frazier's now bisected pant leg, exposing the wound. Blood was streaming out. I put my hands over the wound and pressed down again.

Once again, Frazier screamed.

"I'm sorry," I said.

"It's okay," Frazier said through clenched teeth. "Am I going to be okay?"

"Yeah," I said. "You're going to be okay."

I had no way of knowing that for sure, but I wasn't about to add to Frazier's trauma by revealing my own uncertainty.

I looked up at Wags, who was still holding his hand under Frazier's head.

"Wags, take your jacket off, ball it up and put it under his head," I said.

"Okay," Wags said.

He looked over at Jim.

"Take his head for a minute."

Jimbo slid his hand under the back of Frazier's head again. Wags pulled off his jacket and rolled it up. As he was stuffing it under Frazier's head, I looked up at Jimbo.

"Do you have a first aid kit in that backpack?"

"Yeah," Jimbo said.

He got up and grabbed his backpack.

"I need a bandage," I said.

Jimbo reached into his pack, pulled out a metal box and opened it. Inside he found a large roll of gauze. He held it up.

"This?" he said.

"Yeah. Unroll it. The three of us are going to wrap it around his leg."

I took my hands off of Frazier's thigh and wiped them on my shirt.

"Hold the end," I said to Jimbo.

Jimbo held the end of the roll, as Wags and I took turns wrapping it around Frazier's thigh. We wrapped it around several times, until the bandage ran out.

"Now I need something bigger to wrap around the bandage — a shirt or a jacket," I said.

Jimbo pulled off his jacket.

"Okay," I said. "Lay that out and fold it over on itself. Make it as long as you can and about a foot wide."

Jimbo and Wags laid the jacket down on the rock and followed my instructions.

"Good," I said. "Now let's wrap that around the bandage."

The three of us did that together.

"Now we need something to snug it up," I said. "Jimbo, give me your belt."

I wrapped his belt around Frazier's leg a couple of times, crisscrossing it, pulling it snug, but not too tight, then tucked the buckle under the belt to fasten it as securely as I could.

"We need to get him to a hospital," I said.

"How are we going to do that?" Wags said.

"Wags, you'll run back down to the visitors center and have the ranger call for an ambulance. Jimbo, you and I will carry Frazier down there."

No one moved. I looked at Wags and said, "Go!"

Wags got up and started running down the trail.

"Jimbo, we're going to have to figure out a way to carry him."

"We can't do that," Jimbo said.

"What do you mean?"

"It's too awkward for the two of us to carry him, and we might hurt him. I'll carry him, Andy."

Jim was six foot four and weighed 220. At 33, he was still as strong as a horse, even without the lower half of his right leg, which he'd left in Vietnam. But the two-mile trail back to the parking lot was winding, uneven and steep. I wasn't sure this was a good idea.

"Are you sure you're up to this?"

"Yeah," Jimbo said. "Help me lift him."

Together, Jimbo and I scooped Frazier up until he was securely situated in Jimbo's arms.

"Are you sure about this, Jimbo?" Frazier moaned.

"Frazier, have I ever let you down?"

"No. I hope you won't start now."

"Grab my backpack," Jimbo grunted as he started down the trail. I grabbed his pack and scrambled to catch up.

Jimbo moved fast. Many times, he nearly lost his footing. I stayed close to steady him.

We passed hikers, coming up, along the way. They asked if they could help, but there was nothing they could do.

About halfway down the trail, it changed from gravel to a boardwalk made of thick wooden beams.

"I need to rest," Jimbo said.

"Give him to me," I said, dropping the backpack.

Jimbo lowered Frazier into my arms. He was too heavy for me to hold him very long. I laid him down on the boardwalk as gently as I could.

Jimbo plopped down on a step. He put his elbows on his knees, leaned forward and rested his head in his hands. I kneeled down over Frazier to inspect our makeshift bandage. Thankfully, the bleeding had stopped.

Jimbo pulled his canteen out of his pack and brought it over to Frazier. He helped him sit up with one hand and lifted the canteen to his mouth with the other.

When Frazier was finished drinking, Jimbo handed the canteen to me. Once I'd taken a drink, Jimbo took the canteen, tilted his head back and took great gulps, water spilling over his cheeks and down his neck.

Then he said, "Let's go."

Together, we picked Frazier up and put him back in Jimbo's arms.

Although the boardwalk was the smoothest surface along the trail, it was the hardest for Jimbo because he had to keep stepping down each descending section and, because he was holding Frazier, he had a hard time seeing his feet. So whenever Jimbo came to a step, he stopped, and I grabbed his arm to steady him and help him down.

Finally, the boardwalk came to an end, and the trail became gravel again. At that point, we had less than a quarter of a mile to go. Jimbo was breathing hard and drenched with sweat, but he kept going. As we approached the visitors center, Wags sprinted up the path to meet us.

"An ambulance is on its way," he panted. "It's coming from Kalispell. It should be here soon."

"Good job, Wags," I said.

Jimbo carried Frazier past the visitors center and down the steps to the parking lot. Wags and I were at his sides, but he took the steps slowly and didn't need our help.

The ambulance still hadn't arrived. Jimbo stood in the parking lot, holding Frazier.

"You can put him down now," I said.

"I've got him, Andy," Jimbo said calmly, his eyes fixed on a mountaintop in the near distance.

A few minutes later, the ambulance pulled in. Two paramedics got out and took Frazier from Jimbo. They put him on a stretcher and lifted him into the back of the ambulance.

I told them I was a doctor and asked if I could ride with Frazier. They said yes, and I climbed in.

"We'll follow you," Wags called after me.

"Okay," I said.

As we pulled away, I looked out the back window and saw Jimbo kneeling on the pavement. Wags was standing next to him with his hand on Jimbo's head.

In the back of the ambulance, a paramedic unwrapped Frazier's leg and redressed the wound, which was still oozing blood. Even the slightest touch of his thigh made Frazier call out.

He grabbed my hand and looked up at me. His face was filled with pain and fear.

"Can you give him some morphine?" I said to the paramedic.

"Yes," he said.

He gave Frazier a shot, and he began to relax almost immediately.

"You're going to be okay," I said.

"Thank you for being with me, Andy," he said, looking into my eyes and squeezing my hand before falling asleep.

It took us an hour and a half to get to the hospital. The emergency room doctor on duty was waiting. I explained I was Frazier's friend and a surgeon in Chicago and asked if I could join for the surgery.

"Okay," he said, looking me over.

With a four-day beard, I guess I didn't look much like a doctor. I'm surprised he didn't ask to see my license.

A nurse helped prepare Frazier for surgery. I put on a gown and a mask and scrubbed up. The emergency room doctor administered a general anesthesia, and we got to work.

Getting a clear look at Frazier's wound under the operating room lights, I realized it just how extensive it was. Muscle, veins and arteries were torn. It took the two of us four hours to knit Frazier's thigh back together.

I was sitting next to him in post-op when he began to come to. He looked over at me.

"Am I okay?" he whispered.

"Yes," I said. "You're going to be fine."

He closed his eyes and smiled. Then he opened his eyes and reached out his hand. I took it.

"Thank you for being with me, Andy."

"We are now honored to hear from dad's longtime friend, Doctor John Anderson," a woman said from the lectern.

I slowly rose to my feet and, leaning on my quad cane, stepped out into the aisle. My hand was shaking. A young man sitting across from me got up and stepped over.

"May I give you a hand?" he said in a loud whisper.

"I'm okay," I said with a smile. "Thank you."

I made my way up the aisle. When I got to the casket, I stopped and placed my right hand on the pall. I closed my eyes and stood there for a moment. I thought of Frazier and Jimbo and Wags too. They were all gone now.

I had prepared remarks. They were folded and tucked into the inside pocket of my suit coat.

But then I heard a voice in my mind say, "Speak from your heart."

I opened my eyes. I carefully stepped up into the sanctuary and made my way to the lectern.

I looked out at all the people gathered, but I could see only Frazier, lying not in his casket but on a stretcher, looking up at me as we bumped and zigzagged our way down through the mountains, squeezing my hand and saying, "Thank you for being with me, Andy."

I reached out to him with my right hand.

"Thank you for being with me, Frazier," I began.

The Field

Our new subdivision had been a big, open field.

Our backyards all ran together, down to the end of the street. Beyond that, the land was still wild, with tall grass, big trees and a shallow creek. As boys, we were drawn to it. We explored it on long summer days. We called it "the field."

The Richardsons lived at the end of our street. In their backyard, at the edge of the field, stood a towering oak.

Mr. Richardson built a treehouse in it. From there, we could see both our neighborhood and the field.

At night, we slept in our red brick homes and dreamed of the field.

Manners

No one knows when they went out of style.

Maybe that's because the change was so subtle at first. People stopped saying *thank you* and *please*. In the busyness of life, few noticed.

Then coarse words began to creep into everyday language. At first, they still had the power to shock, but soon they became the new normal.

Voices grew louder, but people grew used to the din. Only action, outrageous action, designed to provoke, got attention, and getting attention was now the point.

Anyway, for anyone who might still care, at some point, almost imperceptibly, manners went out of fashion.

Retrospective

It all began when James bought a new car, his first in nearly 10 years.

There were so many cool new features — automatic high beams, Apple CarPlay, heated steering wheel. The one he loved most, though, was the blind spot indicator on his side mirrors.

James had heard most car accidents happen from the rear. In fact, he himself had been sideswiped. Now he had plenty of warning. He was convinced his favorite new feature had saved him more than once.

Unfortunately, James became so fixated on what was coming from behind that he began to pay far less attention to what lay ahead.

One day, a flash caught his eye, and he never saw the semi stopped in front of him.

Rose

"For you," you said, handing me a single red rose.

"Thank you," I said, surprised by your sweet gesture.

I wondered where you'd gotten it. You were just a boy. Did you clip it from your mother's garden?

It didn't matter. That day, I began to fall in love with you.

And every time you gave me a red rose, I fell in love with you again.

Once I said, "We can't afford it."

"Love is priceless," you said.

Every week for 65 years, you gave me a red rose. Every time, I fell in love with you more deeply.

Now I slowly approach you and gently lay a single red rose over your heart.

"For you," I say.

SHADOW

Perfect

Maddie was the prettiest baby her family and parents' friends had ever seen. Even strangers stopped and stared. With blond hair, big blue eyes and rosy cheeks, she looked like she belonged on the label of a baby food jar.

Her mother had lots of baby pictures taken at a local studio. The studio featured its photos of Maddie on its website. Her mother sent the link to all her friends.

Maddie grew up beautifully, the most popular girl in her class. But when she hit puberty, her looks began to change. She gained weight, and her slender face grew round. Her blond hair turned brown. She needed braces and glasses.

Some of her classmates began to make fun of her, but Maddie didn't mind. She liked the way she looked.

Her mother, though, was disturbed by Maddie's changing appearance.

"Don't worry," she said. "I can help you."

"But I don't need help, Mom."

"You'll thank me later," her mother said.

She signed Maddie up with a modeling agency.

"I want you to turn her back into model material," she told the lady there.

They put Maddie on a strict diet and rigorous exercise program. They swapped her glasses for contacts and her metal braces for clear plastic aligners. They bleached her teeth, waxed her face and dyed her hair.

Her mother was thrilled by the transformation.

"You'll be a famous model after all," she said.

At her first photo shoot under contract, the photographer made Maddie strike a variety of most unnatural poses. She felt uncomfortable, but she obliged and managed to smile, even though she felt like crying.

"Perfect," the photographer said.

The Cave

As a boy, I spent a week every summer with my family at Cave Lake, nestled in the nearby Appalachian forest. Campsites cost $10 a day. It was the kind of vacation we could afford.

As far as parks and campgrounds go, Cave Lake was pretty simple. But for those of us who lived in the inner city, where trees and green space were scarce, Cave Lake was paradise.

I loved camping, fishing and hiking there and, best of all, exploring Frost Cave.

The mouth of the cave was higher than my house and wider than a bus. A small stream flowed out of it. All kinds of things lived deep inside. Bats and ferns and strange crustaceans called isopods.

By rights, we shouldn't have ventured in far enough to see such things. A sign outside said the entrance was open to visitors but exploration of the rest of the cave was limited to experts.

"We'll be experts by the time we get back," Dad would say as we made our way past other campers and visitors obediently hovering around the entrance.

My siblings and I (Mom never went into the cave with us) turned our flashlights on and slowly followed the old man in. It got dark in a hurry. The hard ground was slippery and pock marked by pools of water. Dad said be careful, who knows how deep they were.

Every sound created an echo. We knew there were bats, but we never heard them. We barely saw them. Dad knew where to look, though: up high, along crevices near the ceiling. We'd train our flashlights up there and, sure enough, there was creepy, hairy movement and the glint of tiny eyes.

"Don't disturb them," Dad would say. "They carry rabies."

The very thought made us keep our flashlight beams and voices low.

"Stay together," the old man would say.

We did our best. But once I was shining my light on what I thought were pale fish in one of the still, dark pools, and the next thing I knew, I was all by myself.

I waved my flashlight all around. There was no one there.

"Hello!" I called out, my voice echoing off the walls.

But no one answered. I knew Frost Cave wasn't really one big cave but a series of interconnected small caves. A person could easily get lost. That's probably why the sign said to stay near the entrance.

I kept calling out, but still no one answered. I scanned the cave with my flashlight, but I saw only rocks, water, ferns and walls. I was tempted to look up, to see if there were any bats. But remembering the rabies, I kept my beam low.

My heart was beating fast. I began to sweat, even though the air was cool and damp. I could hear myself breathing hard.

I wondered where my family was, how they could have left me like this. I thought about trying to find them. But what if I made a wrong turn? I decided to stay put. After all, I knew my dad and my siblings would eventually have to pass by here on their way back out.

I'd always been afraid of the dark. I kept my bedroom door open at night and slept with a nightlight next to my bed. Some of the kids played outside after nightfall. Not me. I was the one who turned lamps on in our house at dusk.

Now I sat down on a big rock, sweeping my flashlight around the empty cave like a searchlight. I was alone, with no one entering the cave and no one returning.

What was I to do? What could I do but sit and occasionally call out, hoping someone would eventually hear me.

I tempted fate and shined my light up high, near the ceiling, where the bats lived. But there was no sign of them, and I realized I had been afraid of something that wasn't there.

Why was I afraid of the dark? I had never asked myself that question. I was just afraid. Maybe because of stories I had heard or things I had seen in movies or ghosts I imagined. I wasn't sure.

I thought about calling out again, but instead I turned my flashlight off. I sat in the dark, in the quiet of the cave. The only thing I could hear was the echo of the sound of water slowly dripping. I was not afraid of water. I loved the water.

The rock I was sitting on had a little dip in it, right where I was sitting. I hadn't noticed that before. Not that it made the rock any softer, but I felt comfortable there. I felt secure. I was straddling the rock, and the soles of my tennis shoes were flat against the finely pebbled ground. I couldn't see the ground or the water or the cave walls, but I knew they were there, and all of a sudden I felt safe.

I sat there like that, in the dark, for at least 10 minutes. My heart stopped pounding. I stopped sweating. I stopped worrying.

Then I heard voices.

"Ryan!"

It was Dad.

"Ryan!"

"Ryan!"

"Ryan, where are you?"

The voices of my father, my brother and my sisters echoed off the cave walls.

I was going to call out or turn on my flashlight. But I waited for a few moments. Not to cause them any more concern but to sit in the dark just a little longer and to know, from now on, I would be okay.

They All Run Together

"Did you hear the news?"

"What news?"

"About the mass shooting."

"Where?"

"Hmm, let me think."

"You mean in Indianapolis?"

"No, the one last night."

"In Texas?"

"No, that was last week."

"You're not thinking of the one in Wisconsin, are you?"

"Wisconsin? No, that was a while ago."

"Well, I'm not sure then."

"Me either. Sorry I mentioned it."

"No worries. It's hard to keep them all straight."

"I know. They all run together."

"Isn't that sad?"

"Yeah."

Free

The oncoming car was hugging the outer edge of the road. It had slowed to a crawl by the time Brian Quinn finally realized he was over the center line.

In his rear view mirror, he saw the other driver pulling off the road. Brian hoped he was okay, but he didn't stop to find out.

Fifty years earlier, as a senior in high school, Brian had lots of friends, but he didn't have a girlfriend. Not many of the guys did. Brian's friend Jack Kelly was one of the lucky few. He'd been dating Hannah, one of the prettiest girls in their class, for two years.

Brian quietly had a thing for Hannah. Senior year, their lockers were close by. Brian would see her there, alone, between classes. Sometimes he would catch her eye. He would smile and nod. At first, she would look away, but eventually she smiled back.

One day, Brian stepped over and engaged Hannah in small talk. She seemed eager to talk. Brian was a little surprised, given she had a boyfriend. He even looked around for Jack, but there was no sign of him.

Not that he was afraid of Jack. Everyone knew Jack was a "softie," a sensitive kid who wouldn't hurt anybody. Some kids even said he was a little crazy.

Hannah seemed to quite enjoy when Brian would come over to her locker. When he spoke, she would gaze into his green eyes and smile. Sometimes she would touch his sleeve. Once she even gave him a hug.

"I know you have a boyfriend," Brian said to her one day. "But would you consider going out with me?"

He assumed she'd say no.

But she said, "I'd love to."

Brian was thrilled. He took Hannah to dinner and a movie that Saturday night.

When Jack found out, he was devastated. Hannah tried to console him, but he was beyond consolation. He grew distant from Hannah and everyone. He began getting to school late and leaving early. One day, he didn't show up at all. That evening, Brian learned that Jack was in the hospital. He'd slit his wrists that day.

Brian blamed himself for Jack's misfortune. I should never have moved in on Hannah, he thought. I should have known Jack was fragile and couldn't take it. Brian wanted to visit Jack in the hospital, but he felt too guilty, so he stayed away.

Graduation was just a month away, but Jack never came back to school because he was admitted to a psychiatric hospital. That summer, Brian thought again about visiting Jack, but he still couldn't bring himself to do it.

That fall, when Brian left for college, Jack was still in the hospital. Brian thought about him often. The more he did, the more guilty he felt. Even when he learned Jack had been released, Brian was racked with guilt. He had nightmares about Jack cutting his wrists. He couldn't sleep. He began missing classes. His grades slipped. He started drinking.

After finishing his freshman year with a 1.0 GPA, Brian dropped out of college. He got a job on a construction crew. That summer, he heard that Jack was leaving for college out of state in the fall. He thought about going to see him, but he was still too filled with guilt.

Once he'd left for college, Jack didn't come back to town much. Brian never left. He never went back to school. He never dated or got married. For the next 40 years, he worked on construction crews. Over all those years, with every board he cut, every nail he hammered, every beam he lifted, Brian thought of Jack.

After college, Jack moved to Minneapolis, where he joined a restaurant group as a market analyst. Jack was bright and hardworking. He rose through the ranks and, at 47, became CEO.

Brian heard Jack still came back to town for their high school reunions. But he never attended those gatherings because, despite Jack's success, Brian still felt bad about causing him to nearly take his life.

After his near miss, Brian drove on. He shouldn't have been driving at all. His license was expired, and he no longer tried to renew it because he knew he probably wouldn't make the cut.

He saw a semi coming toward him in the distance. It was far too big to swerve off the road like that car did. Bryan inched beyond the center line. The truck didn't slow down. When it got close, Brian let go of the steering wheel, and his car veered into the other lane.

Three days later, Brian woke up. He was lying in bed in a hospital room, casted, bandaged and hooked up to all kinds of tubes. His whole body ached. He moaned.

"You're awake," someone said.

Brian tried to look to his left, where the man's voice had come from, but he couldn't move his head that far.

"Who's there?" he said.

Brian heard footsteps. Someone was approaching his bed. He looked up. A man stood at the side of his bed, looking down at him. His face looked vaguely familiar. Brian thought maybe he was a doctor.

"What happened?"

"You were in an accident."

"Was the other guy hurt?"

"No, but you're pretty banged up."

"How bad?"

"You'll be in here for a while. But you'll live."

Brian stared into the man's face.

"Who are you?"

"Don't you remember me?" the man said with a smile. "I'm Jack Kelly."

Brian felt his heart skip a beat. It was Jack! Looking up at his wrinkled face, he thought of how he had once driven him to near destruction. Fifty years of guilt seized his brain and tore at his soul. Brian began to cry. His body began to shake.

Jack took hold of Brian's bandaged hand.

"It's okay," he said softly. "It's okay."

Soon a nurse came in and gave Brian more pain medication. This made him drowsy. He fell asleep looking up at Jack, who was smiling and still holding his hand.

When Brian awoke, Jack was still there. It was dinnertime, and Brian was hungry. He ordered some food, which Jack fed him.

The two men talked, each telling the other about his life, about all that had happened since they'd last seen each other in high school.

Then Brian said, "I'm sorry."

"For what?"

"For taking Hannah away," Brian said with tears in his eyes. "For causing you to almost take your own life."

"Oh, Brian. You didn't cause that. I was mentally ill. I'd been ill for years. Yes, I was upset after Hannah went out with you. But I really didn't want to kill myself. I needed help, but I didn't know what to do. I was desperate. Cutting myself was a cry for help. After that, I finally got the help I needed. I still struggle with depression, but I'm getting the therapy I need."

"But you're so successful," Brian said.

"Yes, but that's only because I've had lots of help. I decided to help others too. I made addressing mental illness our corporate cause. Did you know that?"

Brian shook his head.

"Yeah. We've given millions of dollars to help people struggling with mental illnesses. We've made a big difference, and none of it would have happened if not for you. I'm only sorry it's taken me so long to thank you. When I heard about your accident, I came right away, hoping I was not too late."

Real News

Brandon had the *New York Times* delivered daily but never read it. He laid it on his drawing room coffee table to impress his friends, although fewer of them had been dropping by.

Most of his guests never made it to his drawing room. They were captivated by the Kiefer painting in his entryway. They lingered over canapés in his black and chrome kitchen or the drinks he mixed from his fully stocked bar.

Lately, though, no one came by. One Sunday morning, Brandon sat alone, eyeing the Tiffany floor lamp he never liked. Looking down, he reached for the paper.

Hunkered Down

At last, it was over. No more deadly virus. No more need for masks. No more forced isolation.

When the pandemic hit, everyone scurried for cover. Life changed overnight. No more working in offices or learning in classrooms. No more going to movies or holiday gatherings. No more travel.

What an adjustment. At first, it was all so stressful. But then people grew accustomed to living online. They grew accustomed to social distancing. They even grew accustomed to solitude.

In the back of their minds, people remembered how crowded and hectic their lives had become before the virus. They were overextended, worn out. So many relationships had become fractious. Entering the world every day was like preparing to do battle.

So now that the pandemic had come to an end, most people stayed put. They had grown secure in their own little worlds. Why run the risks of venturing out again? Living online isn't so bad. Better to stay hunkered down.

Rain

He watched the rain fall. The forecast had called for sunshine.

It was the fiftieth anniversary of the day he started working. Only he remembered.

He had aspired to greatness. He wanted to become a CEO. Of what, he wasn't sure, but it didn't matter. He simply wanted to be in charge of something big, make a big mark, have people look up to him.

What a foolish dream. In 50 years, he had accomplished nothing of note and had so many low-paying jobs that he was still working.

He watched the rain fall. The forecast had called for sunshine.

Ransom

Jack Lohman grabbed his doctor's bag from the overhead and hurried off the plane. Stepping into the terminal, he pulled out his phone and called Gene Bolser, the president of First National Bank in Chicago.

"Mr. Bolser's office. May I help you?"

"Good morning. May I speak with Gene, please?"

"I'm sorry, but Mr. Bolser is in a meeting. May I take a message and have him call you back?"

"No. It's an emergency. This is Doctor Jack Lohman. Please interrupt him and tell him I'm calling. I'll wait."

"All right, Doctor. I'm going to put you on hold for a moment, but Mr. Bolser will be right with you."

"Thank you."

Jack looked around. He couldn't recall the last time he was in Kansas City.

"Hello, this is Gene Bolser. Jack, are you there?"

"Gene, I'm sorry to interrupt you."

"Is everything okay?"

"I'm fine, but I need your help."

"Sure, Jack."

"I need you to transfer some money from my savings account to the First National Bank in Kansas City, Kansas right away."

"Of course. How much do you need?"

"One million dollars."

 Silence.

"I'm sorry, Jack. Would you repeat that?"

"I said one million dollars."

"One million?"

"Yes, Gene. It's a gift for a friend, and it's urgent. Can you do it?"

"Technically, yes, but I've never—"

"Then do it, Gene. Do it right now. I've just landed in Kansas City. I'll be at the bank in 30 minutes. Oh, and I'll need it in cash."

"Cash?"

"Is that a problem?"

"No, provided they have that much cash on hand."

"Let's hope they do."

"Jack, did you say this is a gift?"

"Yes."

"You know there are tax implications."

"Gene, just do it. We'll work out the tax implications later. Okay?"

"All right, Jack. But when you come back, we need to sit down and talk."

"We will, Gene. Thanks for doing this. Goodbye."

When Jack got to the bank, the manager was waiting along with two armed guards. Paul signed for the withdrawal, then handed over his empty medical bag to be filled with the cash.

"Are you sure we can't deliver it for you?" the manager asked.

"I'll be fine," Jack said. "Thank you."

Sighing, he handed Jack's well-worn bag to one of his bank officers. The manager quietly asked him to go into the safe and fill it with a million dollars in stacks of $100 bills. The two armed guards went with him.

About 10 minutes later, the officer came back and handed Jack's bag to the manager.

"May we help you to your car with this, Doctor Lohman?" the manager said.

"Yes, that would be very helpful. Thank you."

The manager followed Jack, with the armed guards close behind. When they got outside and Paul opened the back door of the taxi, the manager said, "You don't have a car?"

"This is my ride," Jack said. "Just throw that in the back seat."

The manager's face went pale, but he swung the bag into the back seat.

"Thank you," Jack said, shaking the manager's hand.

Then he opened the back door of the cab on the other side and got in.

Jack arrived at his old friend Jim Barlowe's house about 15 minutes later. A police car was parked in the driveway. Jack paid the fare and grabbed his bag.

As Jack walked up the driveway, a policeman got out of his car.

"May I help you?" he asked.

"Good morning, officer. My name is Jack Lohman. I'm here for Mrs. Barlowe."

"Yes," the policeman said. "She's expecting you. Go ahead."

As Paul walked up the driveway, the front door opened. Linda Barlowe, Jim's wife of more than 40 years, was standing in the doorway. She was crying.

"Oh, Jack," she sobbed.

Jack stepped briskly up to the porch, dropped his bag and embraced her.

"It will be okay," Jack said.

Forty years of the vagaries and uncertainties of surgery had taught Jack the wisdom of never telling his patients' loved ones "it will be okay." But in that moment, there seemed nothing else to say.

They held each other for a moment, then he followed her inside.

"Let's sit in the family room," she said.

They sat down on opposite ends of the sofa.

"Thank you for being here," Linda said.

"Thank you for calling me. Have you heard anything more?"

"The police called just before you got here. They said there's nothing new."

"And the kidnappers said they would call you today?"

"Yes. I've been waiting by the phone."

"I called Tony last night," Jack said. "He said he'd try to get a flight out this morning. I suspect he'll be here this afternoon."

Linda looked at Jack.

"Why would someone try to kidnap Jim?"

"He's a wealthy man," Jack said. "Some people would do anything for money."

"I guess you're right. I just hope they don't hurt him."

Jack hadn't seen Linda for two years. She looked as lovely as ever but so much older. He wondered how much of that was due to the strain of the past 12 hours.

"Linda, there is something I need to tell you."

"What?"

"I stopped at a bank downtown on the way here."

"Why?"

"This morning, I had some money wired from my bank to one here in Kansas City."

Linda looked confused.

"Why?"

"Linda, I had a million dollars transferred from my account in Chicago. I have a million dollars in cash in my bag. When the kidnappers call you today, I'm going to drop the money wherever they tell you to drop it, and we're going to get Jim back."

"No! You can't do that!"

"Why?"

"Because Detective Culver said paying ransom is against police policy. Jack, you shouldn't have done this."

He reached over and took her hand.

"Linda, we've got to do everything we can to get Jim back and get him back quickly. I don't know much about kidnapping. But I know that time is not on our side. If these guys want a million dollars to let Jim go, let's pay it. It's just money."

"But this isn't just about money, Jack. We have to listen to the police."

Jack drew a deep breath.

"Linda, after the war, once Jim was better, we were talking about his experience in Vietnam. He was still pretty torn up about those bombing missions. I tried to tell him he was just following orders. He said that most of the time, it's right to follow orders. But sometimes you know in your heart it's not right, and then you have to listen to your heart. When you told me about that police policy last night, I heard you. But then I listened to my heart. That's why I got the money. I know that paying this ransom is the right thing to do, and you've got to let me go through with it."

The phone rang. Linda gasped and sat straight up.

"It's them," she said.

She picked up her phone.

"Hello. Yes, this is Alice Barlowe."

She looked over at Jack, then down at his medical bag.

"Yes, I have the money. Is my husband there? Is he okay? Can I speak to him?"

She looked at Jack as she listened intently.

"Observation Park. Yes, I know where that is. Thirty minutes? Yes, I can be there in 30 minutes. I won't. Are you sure my husband is okay? When will he be released? All right. I'll leave right away. I have the money in a bag, a doctor's bag. I'll put it right where you said."

She hung up, fell back into the sofa and closed her eyes.

"What did they say?" Jack said.

"He said Jim is okay, and I should leave the money between a mailbox and a trash can at the corner of Holly and 21st Streets on the west side of downtown. There's a park there, Observation Park. He said not to call the police. He said if we leave the money, Jim will be released, unharmed, later today."

"Do you have a car here?"

"Yes."

"How long will it take me to drive there?"

"About 20 minutes."

"Okay. I'm going to take your car. About 15 minutes after I leave, I want you to call the police and tell them what's going on. That should give me enough time to drop off the bag. The police should be there when the kidnappers show up."

"Are you sure about this?"

"Yes."

As he backed Linda's car out of the driveway, Jack pulled alongside the police car and gave the officer inside a little wave. He didn't look amused.

It took Jack less than 20 minutes to get to the park. He slowly turned the corner from Holly Street onto 21st. On the corner were a mailbox and an elevated trash can, separated by just a few feet.

Jack found a parking spot about half a block beyond the corner. He got out, opened the back door and pulled out his doctor's bag. Then he walked back to the corner and put it down between the mailbox and the trash can.

He looked around. There were a few people on the sidewalks and some kids and moms in the park but no sign of anyone who looked like a kidnapper.

He started to walk back to Linda's car when he heard the screech of a car's tires behind him. He turned around. At the corner, he saw a dark blue sedan lurch to a halt at the curb. A man was sitting in the driver's seat. Another man jumped out and grabbed the bag. He opened the rear door, yelled something to the driver and threw the bag inside. Just as he did, but before he could even close the door, Jack saw lights flashing and heard sirens blaring all around him.

With the rear door of the car still open and his partner still standing on the sidewalk, the driver took off. The open door hit a car parked just ahead. Jack stepped off the sidewalk and onto the grass as two police cruisers blocked the would-be getaway car's escape and the man who had thrown the bag into the car ran the other way.

Less than a minute later, the police were arresting the driver. A few minutes after that, Jack saw several officers escorting his partner in handcuffs back toward the police cruisers.

A policeman approached Jack.

"You'll have to come with us to police headquarters to file a report," the officer said, looking grim.

"Should I drive?" Jack said.

"Not a chance, buddy. You'll ride with us."

When they got to the station, an officer put Jack in a room and told him to wait there until someone could take his statement.

"Is Jim Barlowe okay?" he asked.

"We don't know yet," the officer said.

Jack sat at a table in the otherwise empty room and waited about 45 minutes for someone to come back in. When an officer finally appeared, Jack again asked, "Is Jim Barlowe okay?"

"Yes. Those two thugs confessed and told us where they were keeping him, just a couple miles away. He's fine."

"Thank God," Jack said. "Does his wife know?"

"Yeah. We just called her."

After Jack gave his statement, he was released. An officer drove him back to Linda's car, which was still parked where he'd left it.

He got in and drove back to the Barlowe's house. A car was parked in the driveway. Jack parked alongside it.

He walked up to the front door. Just as he was about to knock, the door opened. There stood his old friend Jim.

"Jack," he said, embracing him.

Jim was shaking and crying.

"Thank you, my friend," he whispered.

"You would have done the same for me," Jack said.

They went into the family room. Linda, Jack and Jim's old friend Tony Paolino and a man in a suit were all sitting there. Linda jumped up and gave Jack a big hug.

When she finally let go, Tony grabbed Jack and gave him a big hug too.

"Our hero," Tony said.

Jack laughed.

"We were just finishing our statements," Linda said to Jack. "Have a seat."

Jack sat down in an armchair and listened to Jim describe his harrowing day in captivity. When he was finished, the man in the suit, a police detective named Culver, said, "I think I have what we need. Does anyone else have anything to add?"

No one said anything.

"Okay then," Culver said, getting up.

He looked at Jack.

"Doctor, may I have a word with you in the kitchen?"

Jack looked as though he were being called to the principal's office. He got up and walked toward the kitchen. Tony got up too and followed him.

When all three of them were in the kitchen, Culver leaned back against the counter, folded his arms and stared at Jack.

In a low voice, he said, "What you did today, doctor, was very unwise."

Jack looked at him and said nothing.

"Mrs. Barlowe told me that she had told you about our policy not to pay ransom in kidnapping cases. You were aware of that policy, right?"

"Yes," Jack said.

"Doctor, if something had gone wrong, you know you could have been held in contempt."

"I don't care—" Jack started to say.

"He knows," Tony said.

"I'm just glad for everyone's sake that this worked out well," Culver said.

"Me too," Jack said.

Culver continued to stare Jack down. He clenched his jaw and exhaled loudly through his nose. As he turned to leave, Jack looked at Tony and winked.

Jim, Jack and Tony had known each other more than 40 years. They'd met as freshmen in college. Some friendships wane over time, but theirs had only grown stronger and deeper.

After dinner, over beers, the three of them caught up on their lives. But they didn't talk about the kidnapping. Jack and Tony well remembered the trauma Jim had suffered in Vietnam. Through therapy, he had learned to manage it, but it was always there, just under the surface. They didn't want to add to the stress he had experienced over the past 24 hours.

After one beer, Jim got up.

"I'm sorry to do this, guys, but I'm wiped out," he said.

"Get some rest," Jack said.

"Yeah, we'll see you in the morning," Tony said.

Jim gave them each a long hug, whispering thank you, and went to bed.

Jack and Tony grabbed another beer from the fridge and moved to the sunroom so they wouldn't disturb Jim and Linda.

"So what happened today?" Tony said.

Jack recounted the events of that day, from withdrawing a million dollars from the bank to the kidnappers' comical, failed getaway. Even to him, it sounded almost unbelievable.

"You know that detective was right," Tony said. "What you did today was pretty crazy. Why did you do it?"

Jack smiled and took a swig of beer.

"Did you know we categorize heart surgeries by their level of risk?"

"No."

"Yep. Of course, every surgery is risky. But the reality is that very few cases are considered high-risk. What I've learned is that the greatest risk has nothing to do with surgery."

"What do you mean?"

"The greatest risk is waiting too long to act."

Tony looked at his old friend and smiled.

"So you got the money," he said.

"Yeah," Jack said. "I didn't know if it was going to work. But Jim's life was hanging in the balance, and I sure as hell wasn't going to wait."

Charley

I wrapped you in your favorite blanket and laid you in the ground as gently as I could. We said a prayer and threw in handfuls of dirt. I covered you with earth and placed a heart-shaped stone over you.

I know it was time, but letting you go was the hardest thing I've ever done. I know it was right, but it sure doesn't feel right.

For 14 years, you were always there for me, always happy to see me. I want you to know I love you. I beg your forgiveness. I hope to see you and hold you again.

No More Statues

It began in the South. Statues erected long ago to honor men once considered valiant were surrounded, lassoed and pulled down by angry mobs because it was now obvious these men had fought for unjust causes and to honor them was to sanction injustice.

One by one, statues were toppled. There was some resistance. But the beliefs of these statued men were now so abhorrent that anyone standing in the way was vilified and shouted down.

Soon the statues of men who were now seen on the wrong side of history were all gone. But then other statues began to be defaced or destroyed. Statues of men who were once considered inspiring but whose faults were now better understood. These men were not saints but sinners, and to allow their statues to stand was now seen as immoral.

And so, throughout the land, these statues too were removed. Even the statues of men once considered heroes were taken away because they had held opinions or committed acts which were at odds with contemporary thinking and sentiment. No one so flawed, not even a hero, belongs on a pedestal.

Eventually, of course, every statue was torn down because all men are imperfect and no one could pass the test, not even the saints.

All the while, injustice continued. People kept sinning because only the landscape, not their hearts, had changed.

Thinly Veiled Anger

Masked shoppers queued up in a self-checkout line that stretched back to the toilet paper.

Other shoppers needed to get through the main aisle, but nobody in the self-checkout line budged. Trying to squeeze through, a woman clipped a man standing in line. He wheeled around and shoved her cart.

Somebody pushed him. Somebody yelled. Somebody threw a punch.

The self-checkout line broke up. Masked shoppers began running out of the store with items tucked under their arms. Somebody knocked over a clerk. A security alarm sounded.

The manager had to call the cops to restore order.

Together

John and Christine met in their twenties in a shoe store in Manhattan. From the moment their fingers touched over a single shoe, they knew they were destined to be together.

A year later, they pledged their lives to one another. Ten years later, still childless and weary of the big city, they decided to start fresh. For years, they had dreamed of Alaska. Now they ventured there by train to make a new home.

They had a cabin built on the shore of Auke Bay. From their front porch, they watched glaciers calving, great frozen endpoints, once liquid, breaking free and returning to their origin.

For 40 years, they lived there simply, quietly and happily. They both taught at the local campus of the University of Alaska until they retired. They were inseparable.

Then one November, Christine became ill, very ill. John brought her to doctors in Juneau, but they could do nothing for her, so he brought her home.

As the snow began to fall, John cared for Christine day and night, but she grew ever weaker. For each of them, the thought of losing the other was nearly unbearable. In their suffering, they were fused.

In the spring, a neighbor went to their cabin to check on them, but they weren't there. Then he discovered a single set of deep footprints in the soft soil from their front steps to the water's edge.

Choices

"I love you," he said. "I want to marry you, but I have one condition."

"What's that?"

"We must never hit our children."

She laughed.

"I'm serious. If you ever hit our children, I'll leave you and take them with me."

She looked into his eyes and saw a pain she hadn't seen there before.

"Okay."

They raised their children with kindness and respect. They grew up to be confident and open-hearted. Now they're raising their own children as they were raised.

His granddaughter giggles. I didn't laugh much as a kid, he thinks. His choices make him happy.

Regret

He gets up early every morning, makes himself a cup of coffee and sits longways on the sofa in his family room alongside two large windows in the back of his house.

It's always dark when he gets up. In the winter, he used to watch the sky lighten and a line of trees in the nearby woods emerge, all hardwoods except for one big evergreen.

There was something about that evergreen that bothered him. It seemed out of place. It just didn't fit.

One day, he went into the woods with a chainsaw. He made his way to the evergreen, a stout, 40-foot Norway spruce, and cut it down at the base. It was far too big to drag away, so he sliced off the branches and cut the trunk into pieces, which he carried home for firewood.

These days, he sits on the opposite end of his sofa in the morning. He doesn't want to face the hardwood trees, which now look monotonous and lonely, like stalwart soldiers standing at perpetual attention in honor of a fallen comrade. The very sight of them fills him with regret.

Short Memories

The virus spread. Everyone hunkered down. Leaders reacted unevenly. Factories closed. The economy tanked.

Eventually, the virus went away, and the world was changed.

People realized how much they loved being together and even going to work.

The air cleared, and governments took a fresh look at climate change.

The economy bounced back. Bricks and mortar, and strong leadership, still mattered.

People remembered that being fully human means having real contact with other human beings.

But as the pandemic faded, the world reverted to its old ways. Until the next time, when it learned the same lessons again.

Wild Child

Justin was a wild child. That's what people called him anyway. Free spirit. Did what he wanted. Talked back. Skipped school. Ran around barefoot in thunderstorms. Gave his parents fits.

"Behave," his mother pleaded.

"Go to your room," his father demanded.

But Justin wouldn't change. In desperation, his mother took him to a doctor, who prescribed medicine, which settled him. Helped him study, get good grades. No more back talk. No more running around in the rain. Straight As. Scholarship. College. Job. Wife. Kids.

"Liam's a wild child," Justin's wife said.

"Let him be," said Justin, watching the dark clouds move in.

Escape

The old man felt like a prisoner in his tiny apartment. His only excitement these days was a knock on his door when a faceless worker would bring a meal and leave it on a bench in the hallway. No visitors allowed.

He had felt lonely before the pandemic. Now his loneliness had become unbearable.

He'd watched the snow fall for three days. The small patch of land that was his yard was now a harbor of pure white. The alabaster trees just beyond beckoned him.

He zipped up his coat, slid open the patio door and waded into the deep snow. The frigid air stung his nostrils. The brilliant sun hurt his eyes. The stiff wind nearly blew him over.

At last, he felt alive.

The Strain

They thought they had conquered it, but it came back. It always comes back.

They used science to battle it. They took every measure, used every weapon, developed new weapons. But it would not go away. It kept advancing. It invaded every part of society, from dark alleys to places of worship.

Until then, they considered the virus their most formidable foe. But the virus went away.

Extremism remained. It is still advancing. It is a particularly virulent strain of disease, impervious to both medicine and reason, and as long as it has a willing host, it cannot be eradicated.

LIGHT

Sun

I look out this window every morning. Sometimes it's still dark when I get up and sit here with my coffee.

I like to watch the sun rise. I can't actually see the sun from where I sit, but it doesn't matter. I see clouds appear in the bright sky. I see trees — green, red and purple — shimmer in a light from the East.

The trees and clouds were here when I awoke, and they'll be here tonight when darkness falls. I won't see them, but I'll know they're here because of the light of a sun I don't see.

New and Improved

When I was a kid, we had a 1962 Rambler. It was black with a red interior and a steering wheel that looked like it belonged on a bus. No seat belts. Sitting in back was like sitting on your sofa if your sofa was upholstered in stiff vinyl. It sounded like a truck. The tailpipe spewed blue clouds of exhaust.

Last spring, I bought a new car. It's a hybrid. Lots of features. I'm still trying to figure out how to operate it. It's usually quiet, but sometimes an alarm sounds. I'm not sure why or what I should do.

Undeserved

Last fall, I found a packet of wildflower seeds in my garage. I went out back, tore it open and sprinkled the seeds over a bare spot along the fence.

I was in a hurry that day. I didn't rake the soil or water. The packet of seeds was old, and I knew it was a long shot that I'd see any flowers anyway. At least the birds will eat, I thought.

I forgot all about those seeds until this spring, when I looked out my window one morning and saw a splash of purple, yellow, blue, white and red.

Live Oak

Kiara always loved trees. Her earliest memories were of watching her brothers climb a big sycamore in their backyard.

She remembered them scaling it by grabbing hold of the huge trunk and stepping up little boards their father had nailed up. She remembered them disappearing into the branches and staying up there for what seemed a very long time, calling her name.

They knew she couldn't climb up after them. She was too young. Even as she grew, Kiara wasn't able to climb that sycamore or any other tree for that matter. She could never manage to scale a tree trunk.

But one day when she was eight, Kiara came upon a massive oak tree in the woods near her house. It was unlike any tree she had ever seen. Its lowest limbs nearly touched the ground, extending from its great trunk like giant arms.

Kiara leaned over one, belly high. She swung her left leg up over it and sat up, straddling it. Then she crouched on the enormous limb, grabbed a sturdy branch above her and pulled herself up.

For the first time, she was climbing a tree! Exhilarated by her ascent, she made it all the way to the top, where she looked out over all the other trees, even a few sycamores.

Kiara felt dizzy but safe in the arms of the tree. She felt as if she had been lifted up to the sky. She imagined herself as an angel, looking down on all of creation.

When she got home, Kiara told her mother about the special tree she had found.

"That's a live oak," her mother said.

"A live oak? Aren't all oak trees alive?"

"Yes, but a live oak stays green all winter."

"How does it do that?"

"It holds onto its leaves and drops them in the spring."

Kiara thought about telling her brothers. Maybe they'd want to climb this special tree too. But they were teenagers now and had lost interest in climbing trees.

But Kiara never lost interest in that live oak. She climbed it as a teenager. It was the last thing she did before she left home and moved away.

Now Kiara is old, and her parents and brothers are gone. Every summer, she goes back to the woods near her old house. The live oak is still there. Slowly, cautiously, careful not to disturb its leaves, Kiara climbs to the top.

She is mindful this is the only tree she has ever climbed. She feels so grateful for this old tree. She remembers the day she first saw it. She wonders if she found it or it found her.

Kiara, now old like the tree, holds fast to its branches. She feels dizzy but safe. She looks out over all creation and imagines she's an angel.

Appreciation

She browsed the artwork around the room where her painting was newly hung. Her soul was in this painting. She considered it her finest work yet, and she was eager to see the other museumgoers' reactions.

But as people stepped by it, giving it only a passing glance, her heart sank. Had she missed the mark? Had she lost her touch?

She sat down on a bench in the center of the room. She watched a young man approach her painting. He stopped and studied it. After a few minutes, he slowly backed away and sat beside her, his eyes still fixed on her creation.

He sat there silently, then whispered, "That speaks to me."

Sunrise

Haiti awoke in the darkness. She slipped out of her small house and headed for the beach. She would be back in less than an hour, before her daughter and husband awoke.

She followed a dirt path, the moon lighting her way. Like old friends, the waves softly called her name.

She slipped off her sandals. The morning air was warm, and the sand felt cool on the soles of her feet. She sat down where the sand was soft and dry.

Haiti closed her eyes and whispered a prayer, then opened her eyes just in time to watch the sun rise, as she did every day.

The Somnolence of Routine

Wearing a gray suit, as always, Jonathan Beedle unlocked the front door of the Second National Bank and pulled it open, just as he had every morning, Monday through Saturday, for 13 years.

As branch manager, he took his duties seriously, opening the bank just before nine and locking up precisely at five.

His employees saw him every morning when they arrived, every evening when they left and every Sunday in church. He never missed a day.

Except the Monday morning when he didn't show up, the day the police found the bank vault empty, the day they went looking for Jonathan Beedle.

The Pill

"The Pill" wasn't advertised. Word of mouth and five-star reviews were enough to drive millions in sales.

Its manufacturer, DAE, claimed taking just one pill a day, combined with light exercise and modest calorie reduction, could enable a person to lose two pounds a week.

Customers loved it. "It's a miracle," many said. Several posted before and after photos to show off their 100-pound weight loss in less than a year.

The Pill was rated one of the best weight-loss products of all time. Then it was discovered it was a placebo and DAE stood for "diet and exercise."

Saved

The homes in my neighborhood were built 50 years ago. Only one of the original residents still lives there. His name is Bill Harper. He lives three doors down.

Bill lives alone. His wife died last year. Until recently, I hadn't met him.

I don't know most of my neighbors. Until the pandemic, I wasn't home much. I'm in sales, and I used to travel four days a week. But with everyone hunkering down and hardly anyone flying, I've been working from home.

It's been strange. Before, I set up appointments and called on customers. Now I live on Zoom.

It's been a big adjustment. Not just the work. But where I work and even where I live. I feel like a stranger in my own house. My wife and kids are driving me crazy. They're noisy, and they're always interrupting me. I lock the door to my office upstairs, but they still manage to get in. Some days, I can't get anything done.

Lately, I've been taking walks just to get away. It's quiet in the neighborhood. With the pandemic, everyone's inside. I like that. No need for small talk.

A few weeks ago, I went out for a walk. I was walking by Bill Harper's house when I heard someone call, "Good morning."

I looked over and saw Bill sitting on his front porch. He was wearing pajamas and reading the newspaper.

"Good morning," I said.

"Beautiful day."

"Yes, it is."

I smiled, gave him a little wave and kept walking. I'd almost passed his driveway when he called, "Got a minute?"

I didn't want to be rude, so I stopped.

"Sure," I said.

"I've got a quick question, if you don't mind."

So much for my quiet walk, I thought.

I walked up his driveway. Bill got up and laid the newspaper down. He was tall and thin. I knew he was old. I'd seen him, driving by his house, many times. Now, close up, he looked even older. His face was drawn, and his pajamas hung on him like a farmer's clothes on a scarecrow.

As I approached, he pulled a face mask out of his pocket and put it on.

"Just to be safe," he said.

"Oh, yeah," I said, pulling my mask out and slipping it on.

We stood there, two masked strangers, looking at each other for an awkward moment. I wondered what he wanted.

"I'm sorry to bother you," he said. "Do you know how to use Zoom?"

"Yeah."

"Well, Carol has — had — a computer, but I really don't know how to use it. I was wondering ..."

"Would you like me to show you how to use Zoom?"

"Yes. But if now's not a good time ..."

"Now is fine."

"Oh, good. Please come in. By the way, I'm Bill Harper."

I climbed the two steps to his porch and gave him a gentle fist bump.

"I'm Matt. Matt Jenkins. I live a few doors down."

"It's good to meet you, Matt. I know you're busy. I won't take but a minute of your time."

He turned around and pushed open his front door. I noticed this took some effort.

"Come in," he said.

I followed him into the foyer.

"It's right here," he said, shuffling into the dining room.

Near the edge of the table was a laptop, a MacBook Air. It was open. A power cord dangled from the computer to a wall outlet. The morning sun through the windows filled the room with bright light. Looking around, I noticed a layer of dust on everything.

Bill pressed a button on the keyboard, and the screen lit up.

"I never turn it off. I'm afraid I won't be able to turn it back on. I don't know Carol's password."

"I see. Do you mind if I sit down?"

"Please," he said. "Would you like something to drink? Some coffee?"

"No, thanks," I said, sitting down.

He pulled out a chair at the end of the table and sat down too.

"I'd sit next to you, but, you know," he said.

"I understand. Do you happen to have a Zoom account?"

"No."

I set one up for him.

"I need to show you how to use it. Why don't you sit here?" I said, patting the seat of the chair next to me. It's okay. We're wearing masks."

Bill pulled out the chair and sat down beside me. He folded his hands in front of him on the table. I noticed they were trembling.

I showed him how to set up a Zoom meeting.

"Do you happen to know who you'll be meeting with?" I asked.

"Yes. My children and my grandchildren, I hope. I haven't seen them since before the pandemic."

"Have they come to visit?"

"No. They think it's too risky for me."

"I'm sorry. Well, now you should be able to see them."

"Thank you."

He was staring at the computer. I noticed his eyes were moist.

"Is there anything else I can help you with?"

"No," he said, getting up. "You've been most helpful."

I followed him to the front door. I stepped ahead and pulled it open.

"I can't thank you enough, Matt."

"You're very welcome, Bill. It was good to finally meet you."

I started to give him a fist bump, but he opened his arms and embraced me. Standing back, I saw tears in his eyes.

"Are you okay?"

"Yes," he said, wiping his eyes.

I wanted to know for sure he was all right but didn't want to embarrass him. So I wished him a good day and invited him to call me with any questions.

I walked back down the driveway and took off my mask. I had gone for a walk that morning to be alone. Now solitude seemed so lonely.

I decided not to continue my walk. I went home.

Observe

He felt angry. He still wasn't sure why he'd been sent to this far-away land. None of his colleagues had ever been given a "broad-ening assignment." Did he have some deficit? If so, wasn't there an easier way to get training?

He didn't know how to eat the unfamiliar food in front of him. He watched others in the crowded restaurant. He listened more carefully. He didn't know their language, but he began to get a sense of what they were saying from their facial expressions and tone of voice. He started paying closer attention to everyone around him.

He picked up his chopsticks. Holding them awkwardly in his right hand, he pinched a bite of food and slowly brought it to his mouth.

The Scale

He stepped out of the shower and dried off. Then, as he did every morning, he went over to the scale and stepped onto it.

"Damn," he muttered, just loud enough for his wife to hear from their bedroom.

She knew what that meant. He had either gained a few ounces or hadn't lost the weight he was aiming to lose, the weight he was working so hard to take off. And it meant he would have a bad day.

He grumbled as he trudged by her and went downstairs. She loved her husband. To her, he looked perfect. She had told him that, but he was obsessed with hitting a certain target weight. Falling short threw him into a funk.

She hated to see him this way. So as soon as he'd left for work, she went upstairs and adjusted the scale to read a pound light.

The next morning, she heard her husband get out of the shower, step on the scale and yell, "Woo hoo!" He emerged from the bathroom beaming.

"Good morning," he said, giving her a kiss.

Every once in a while, when her husband wasn't around, she would adjust the scale to read just a bit lighter. She felt a little guilty, but she loved seeing her husband happy.

The Light

Broken and spent, he worked his way through the trees, down to a moonlit river. A ferryman was waiting on a skiff. He climbed on board, and the ferryman pushed off.

The water was calm. The closer they got to the other bank, the more luminous it became.

Finally, the boat reached shore. He stepped off and looked back across the river. The trees, the land he had known, even the water were all fading into the light.

The light now surrounded him. It cradled him. It warmed him. He began to remember it. He began to feel whole again. Then he too faded into the light.

Dorothy

I took my groceries from my cart and placed them on the belt.

I watched a young woman bagging groceries. She was short. Her face was flat, and her head was small. Her eyes were shaped like almonds. Her name tag said Dorothy.

When I was growing up, there was a boy in our neighborhood who looked like this. I never knew his name.

As the cashier scanned my items, I stepped forward to the bagging area.

"May I help you, Dorothy?"

"Sure," she said with a smile.

We stood there, Dorothy and I, side by side, bagging groceries together.

The Gift

James hated shoveling Mrs. Pater's driveway. She never paid him. He'd never even seen her. But his mother made him do it.

She's probably dead in there, James thought, as he trudged down to the old Pater house.

He'd finished her driveway and just finished her porch when the front door opened slightly.

A box wrapped in colorful paper emerged from behind the door. Bony fingers held it.

"For you," said a weak voice inside.

James reached out and took the box.

"Thank you," he said.

"Merry Christmas," said the disembodied voice.

I hope she's okay, James thought, as he carried his gift home.

Waltz of the Flowers

He rode into town on a Harley, wearing leather, tattooed, covered with dust.

He pulled up to the Bulldog Saloon. He planted his left boot in the gravel and swung his right leg over the hog. He looked like The Rock.

He brushed himself off and stepped inside. The place was crowded and noisy. He ordered whiskey.

"No music around here?" he said to the bartender.

"Band starts in an hour."

He looked over at the piano.

"Mind if I play?"

"Go right ahead."

He strode over to the upright, floorboards creaking under his weight. He pulled out the bench with one hand, sat down and began to play.

The patrons grew quiet. It was the first time they'd heard Tchaikovsky's "Waltz of the Flowers."

The Nature of Grace

It's not that Henry had done anything particularly bad that year. He just hadn't done anything very good.

He had plenty of chances. He could have been nicer to his sister or shoveled old Mrs. Peterson's driveway. He simply hadn't made the effort.

So on Christmas Eve, Henry lay in his bed crying because he knew there would be nothing under the tree for him in the morning. He knew he was undeserving.

As the sun came up, Henry awoke to the laughter of his sister in their family room. As he stepped through the doorway, she cried, "Henry! Look at all the gifts for you!"

About the Author

After a long career in the corporate world, Don Tassone has returned to his creative writing roots.

Snapshots is his seventh book. The others are the novels *Francesca* and *Drive* and four short story collections: *New Twists, Sampler, Small Bites* and *Get Back*.

Don and his wife Liz live in Loveland, Ohio. They have four children and five grandchildren.